Freaky

HiP HOP KiDZ®

Freaky

Written by Jasmine Beller

Grosset & Dunlap

GROSSET & DUNLAP
Published by the Penguin Group
Penguin Group (USA) Inc., 375 Hudson Street,
New York, New York 10014, U.S.A.
Penguin Group (Canada), 90 Eglinton Avenue East, Suite 700, Toronto, Ontario,
Canada M4P 2Y3 (a division of Pearson Penguin Canada Inc.)
Penguin Books Ltd, 80 Strand, London WC2R 0RL, England
Penguin Ireland, 25 St Stephen's Green, Dublin 2, Ireland
(a division of Penguin Books Ltd)
Penguin Group (Australia), 250 Camberwell Road, Camberwell, Victoria 3124,
Australia (a division of Pearson Australia Group Pty Ltd)
Penguin Books India Pvt Ltd, 11 Community Centre, Panchsheel Park,
New Delhi - 110 017, India
Penguin Group (NZ), Cnr Airborne and Rosedale Roads, Albany, Auckland 1310,
New Zealand (a division of Pearson New Zealand Ltd)
Penguin Books (South Africa) (Pty) Ltd, 24 Sturdee Avenue, Rosebank,
Johannesburg 2196, South Africa

Penguin Books Ltd, Registered Offices:
80 Strand, London WC2R 0RL, England

Published by Grosset & Dunlap, a division of Penguin Young Readers Group, 345
Hudson Street, New York, New York 10014. GROSSET & DUNLAP is a trademark
of Penguin Group (USA) Inc. Printed in the U.S.A.

Library of Congress Control Number: 2006024528

ISBN 978-0-448-44364-5   10 9 8 7 6 5 4 3 2 1

CHAPTER 1

"**E**merson! Hey, you made it!" Sophie Qian called to her best friend. "Let me give you the scoop. You've got your pizza station over there. Your egg rolls, spring rolls, and other Chinese finger food made by the fingers of my fifth-generation-Chinese mother over there. Your healthy bun-bun food to the left. KFC over yonder. Drinkables in the kitchen. All things sweet and chocolatey to come later."

"Wow." Emerson Lane stepped out of the Miami heat and into the Qians' air-conditioned living room, her long blond hair swishing around her shoulders. "When are a hundred more people showing up to eat all this?"

"It's not just one party," Sophie reminded her. "It's a combo 'Yay, Hip Hop Kidz came in first at the Southeast regionals,' 'Yay, Devane is off probation and is a Hip Hop Kid again,' 'Yay, we're going to the nationals in L.A. in two and a half weeks,' 'Yay, you and ill papi are back in the group,' 'Yay, my sister, Sammi, is now an official Hip Hop Kid' party," she rattled off without pausing for breath. "That's—" She did a quick count on her fingers. "That's five parties going on at once in here. I'm not sure we have *enough* food. Especially because you know some of us like to eat."

Sophie shook her booty and nodded toward Becca Hahn, who was wearing her "I don't skinny-dip, I skinny-dunk," T-shirt, the turquoise one that made her long red hair look extra fiery. "So give me a 'Yay' and go eat. Or dance. We shoved all the living room furniture in the bedrooms to make space for everyone to bust out their best."

"Yay!" Emerson cried. "Actually, I guess that should be 'yay, yay, yay, yay, yay!' One for each thing we're celebrating.

"Uh-huh," Sophie agreed. "With an extra one for you being a hip-hop girl again. I'm so glad your parents let you come back, Em."

"Um, this probably isn't the time to say this. I don't want to make the party less yay-filled." She hesitated.

"Tell me," Sophie urged.

"My parents are only letting me come back until the group goes to the nationals—and the world championship if we get that far. They don't think it's right to penalize the team by pulling me out of Hip Hop Kidz before the competition, when I've been rehearsing with you guys and everything. But as soon as we're back from L.A., that's it. I have to quit. They're still really mad at me."

"Oh, Em, no!" Sophie exclaimed. "There has to be a way

to make them change their minds. Like if we win! If we come back as the world champions, they'll have to let you stay in the group."

"No way. I lied to them. I told them I was going to ballet class every time I went to a Hip Hop Kidz Performance Group rehearsal. I pretended to be sick and snuck out of the house to go to the regional competition. They're never going to forget any of that. It's over, Soph."

Emerson's words did suck some of the fun out of the party. The beats of the new Dilated Peoples track didn't seem so juicy now. Sophie and Emerson had been asked to join the performance group on the same day. And they'd become totally tight. Hip Hop Kidz wouldn't be the same without her.

"That's not what we should be thinking about now," Emerson said. "There's too much to be happy about. We're going to the nationals together. And then we're going on to the world championship—I know it!" She glanced around to make sure no one was listening and leaned a little closer to Sophie. "I think it's so cool that you made part of your party a celebration of Sammi getting in the group. I know that wasn't . . . you know, the best thing that ever happened to you."

"I decided to put my whole jealousy thing with Sammi down the garbage disposal," Sophie admitted. "I mean, so what if she's a cheerleader and on the debate team and in the choir and all those millions of things. Do I want to be a rah-rah for a bunch of meat on legs? No. Do I want to argue for hours about stuff I don't even care about? No. Do I want to sing—okay, well, sort of. But I got my voice from my dad, so I have to stick to the shower."

Emerson laughed.

"I realized the thing I really want to do, I'm doing. I want to dance," Sophie continued.

"Me too," Emerson agreed. "Dance until my feet fall off." She started popping her feet, letting the motion travel all the way up her body. Sophie joined in.

"And I can do that with my sis onstage with me. Actually, it's kind of cool. I love Sammi. Even if she is perfect!" *Especially because ill papi doesn't* like *like her*, Sophie silently added. That made it so much easier not to go all jealous over her sister. It didn't matter that Sammi and Sophie *like* liked the same boy, as long as he didn't *like* like either one of them. His mom and dad had a messed-up relationship—make that non-relationship—so ill papi had decided he only wanted girls as friends. Not girlfriends.

Fridge boogied up to Emerson and did this move he'd made up that was sort of a Frankenstein walk, if Frankenstein had been given Ricky Martin hips when he was created. Sophie found herself face to face with the ills. Fridge's big blocky body had totally hidden him.

Ill papi grinned at Soph. "That pizza was slammin'," he

told her as they danced. "But the cheese was, like, super-elastic. I had the slice stretched all the way to here"—he held his hand up over his head—"and it would not break. It was that gooey. I was like . . ." Ill papi tilted his head back and started poppin' his neck and snapping his jaws, showing her how hard it was to bite through the cheese.

"Nice move," Sophie commented. She started popping her neck and chomping, adding a pulling-snapping motion over her head. "I think we should add this to our routine for the world championship. We'd definitely win."

"You're whack," ill papi told her between jaw snaps.

Sammi didn't know what Sophie and ill papi were doing exactly. Some kind of dance a rabid dog would come up with. But it looked like they were having fun.

She waited for a green-eyed attack. It didn't come. For once she wasn't getting all jealous of her little sister just because ill papi liked hanging with Sophie more. Even though Sammi was older. And prettier. She wasn't being conceited. It was just what everybody knew to be a fact. Sammi and her sister both had the same long black hair, dark eyes, and creamy skin. But Sophie was chubby-cute. And Sammi was hot.

It used to make her feel like her head was going to implode when ill papi chose to hang with Sophie instead of her. The boy had actually turned Sammi down when she asked him out. He didn't even think about it. Just said no.

But now Sammi knew ills wasn't hanging with Sophie in a girlfriend kind of way. He didn't want any girlfriends of any kind. Somehow that made the ill papi/Sophie combo okay. Sammi was used to her little sis having guy friends. Everybody liked Sophie that way.

Sammi smiled. This was good. She felt like somebody had untied the knot in her small intestines.

"You can keep smiling," Ky told her as he approached. "I won't disappoint. I'll ask you to dance."

Sammi snorted. Ky Miggs always came off with these total playa lines. But he could never keep the grin off his face once he got them out of his mouth. He was such a marshmallow, just total sweetness.

"I won't disappoint, either. I'll say yes," Sammi told him.

The music went from pulse-pounding to slow. Ky took her by the waist, and Sammi slid her arms around his neck. Over his shoulder she saw Sophie and ill papi dancing. No pang.

But ill papi was pretty cute. Make that very cute. And his whole no-girlfriend resolution had to change at some point. Didn't it?

Stop, Sammi ordered herself. *Don't start getting all crazy again. He's not interested in you.*

Ky took her in a slow spin, moving ill papi out of her sight.

Ky is interested, Sammi told herself. *He's the kind of guy you should want to be with. He's just as cute as ill papi. Just in a different way. And he's funny. And he's smart.* Ky gave her a dramatic dip, tango-style, as the song ended.

And he can dance.

"Um, do you think—would you want to go to the movies or something sometime? Maybe on Friday?" Sammi asked him as he pulled her out of the dip.

His eyes widened slightly. Then he gave the Ky grin. "I knew you'd be asking me out. No girl can resist the Ky factor."

Sammi shook her head at him. "So is that a yes?"

"Yes," he answered. "Absolutely, yes."

Be happy about this, Sammi told herself. *Ky's great.*

He totally is, she told herself again as her eyes slipped to ill papi for one quick second.

Devane took the first bite of her potato salad, then immediately put her plate down. Maddy Caulder, the head of the Hip Hop Kidz program, and Gina Torres, the teacher of the Performance Group, were back from the kitchen. They were standing in a perfect spot to see the contours she'd been working on.

And she needed them to see her new moves. Because she knew they were going to be figuring out the solos for the nationals really soon. This was her moment. She couldn't pull the contours out in class. Gina expected you to dance Gina's choreography, period. Devane had learned that the very hard way when she had made a little—okay, big—change in a routine during a show, and immediately got slammed into probation hell. Now that she was off probation, there was no way she was risking getting thrown in again.

But there was nothing wrong with breaking out a new move at a party. It was what parties were for. It was just lucky for her that Maddy and Gina happened to be here. And once Maddy and Gina got a demonstration of Devane's tasty contour action, it would make their decision very easy. Solo number one? Devane. Solo number two? Devane. Solo number three? Devane.

Okay, so maybe they'd have to mix it up a little, but after Maddy and Gina saw the new stuff, Devane was definitely getting a big solo, and that meant everyone at the world championship would know who she was. Because they *were* getting to world. With Devane off probation? No doubt.

Devane danced her way over to a spot on the floor near Maddy and Gina, but not directly in front of them. No need to be too obvious. Then she began using her hands to outline the contours of her body in the air in front of her. She could do other objects, too—a sleek cat, a stretch limo. But she liked doing herself the best. What was a better subject than Devane?

Once she'd air-traced herself from her head to her toes, she continued dancing like she had no idea she'd shown the room something burnin'. But the look she saw Maddy exchange with Gina confirmed her suspicions.

Mission accomplished, Devane thought. *Solo locked.*

CHAPTER 2

Emerson studied herself in the mirror over her dresser. She was trying to decide if she looked like the kind of daughter her parents would be proud to introduce to the friends they were having over for dinner.

Well, there was nothing about her that screamed "I dance hip-hop," so that was a start. The words "big fat liar" weren't written across her forehead in big red letters. Also good. But Emerson knew how badly she'd disappointed her mom and dad. She'd never forget the look on her mother's face when Emerson climbed back in her bedroom window after she'd snuck out—after telling about a million lies—to perform in the Southeast Regional Hip-Hop Championship.

Her mother had looked at Emerson like she was a stranger. A stranger she had no interest in getting to know. Even now, weeks later, her mom, and her dad, too, still kind of treated her like a stranger. Very polite. But chilly.

Emerson checked the clock. Five minutes to seven. She needed to get herself downstairs. Being late wasn't a "perfect daughter" kind of thing. Not that she'd ever again be considered a perfect daughter, but she could at least give the outward appearance of one. She smoothed her perfectly smooth French braid, straightened her perfectly straight skirt, and headed downstairs.

"Good. You're ready," Mrs. Lane said when she saw her. Emerson felt like she was being checked off her mom's mental list, along with the freshness of the flowers in the arrangement and the correct blend of seasonings in the carrot soup. She tried not to sigh. At least it meant she'd achieved the outward perfect-daughter look she was going for. Her mother would have sent her back upstairs to change or redo her hair or whatever if she hadn't.

"Is there anything I can do?" Emerson asked. The doorbell rang before she got all the words out.

"You can answer the door and take our guests into the living room," her mom said. And she smiled. She actually smiled. At Emerson. "You look perfect, sweetie."

Emerson smiled back and headed over to the door. She swung it open and gave another smile, the so-happy-you're-here one. "Hello, I'm Emerson. And you're the Douglases, am I right?"

Mr. Douglas, a big bear of a guy with orange hair, grinned at her. "You got it. I'm Frank. This is my wife, Lizette. And my son, Wes."

"Nice to meet you. Come on inside. Let me take your

coats," Emerson volunteered.

After she'd carefully hung the coats—Mr. Douglas, Burberry, tan; Mrs. Douglas, Prada, red, three-quarter length; Wes, leather bomber—in the hall closet, she led the way into the living room.

"I love that painting," Mrs. Douglas exclaimed as she took a seat on the Edra flap sofa Emerson's mother had just replaced their old—one year old—couch with.

"It's a Giorgio Morandi," Emerson told her. "He painted the same basic things, like that bottle and that box, over and over again. Supposedly he was trying to understand reality by painting familiar objects."

"I think we might have an art history professor on our hands," Emerson's dad joked as he came into the room.

"I thought your girl was going to be this country's next prima ballerina," Mrs. Douglas commented as Emerson's mom joined them.

Gulp. Ballet was the absolute most sore subject for Emerson and her parents.

"Well, she did make a perfect snowflake in last year's *Nutcracker*," Mrs. Lane said. Her voice was even and smooth. Her smile stayed on her face. She didn't give any indication that everything about ballet brought up bad memories for her. "She got to perform with the Russian Ballet Company."

"Lovely," Mrs. Douglas said. "Wes played the violin with the Boston Pops at a charity concert."

Emerson glanced at Wes. He didn't look like he minded being in the middle of the battle of the bragging parents. Even when his dad got his violin out of the trunk after dinner and had him play for everybody.

Then again, she probably looked fine with it, too. Even when her mom dragged out the DVD of Emerson's last ballet recital. She had to pretend that the whole night was fun, fun, fun, since she was still going for the outward-perfection thing.

Still, she couldn't stop a long from-the-toes sigh of relief when the last Douglas was out the door and she was finally free to go up to her room.

"Emerson," her mother called when she'd climbed only one stair.

What now? she thought. *Even trained seals get a break, don't they?*

"Wes's mom was telling me that there's a dance coming up at his prep school on Friday. It's all boys. Some girls from another prep school are being invited, but Wes would feel more comfortable if there were a girl there he knew. It'll be the first dance he's ever been to," her mom told her.

Emerson knew what was coming. And she didn't see any way to stop it.

"Mrs. Douglas and I thought it would be nice if you two could go together. It sounds like a good time, don't you think?"

It would make her mom happy. Her dad, too. And it wasn't like Wes wasn't nice. Maybe he was even doing the perfect-son thing. Maybe at the dance, they could both be . . . a little less perfect.

And it wasn't as if Emerson really had a choice. Her mother was acting like she was asking, but she wasn't—she was telling. And after the non-perfect daughter stuff Emerson had done, there was no way she could argue.

"Sure," she told her mom. "I'd like to go to his dance with him."

Devane pushed her way through the main doors of the Hip Hop Kidz building an hour before the Hip Hop Kidz Performance Group was supposed to start. She'd gotten there early partly because her ten-year-old brother, Tamal, was driving her crazy. He was doing a book report on *Because of Winn-Dixie*, and he seemed to feel like telling her every single thing that happened on every single page was a necessary step toward getting it finished. "And the dog, he smiled. And the girl, she was lonely. And the librarian—" Please. Devane had already passed the fifth grade, thank you very much. She was in the seventh. And she knew the book better than he did. She'd only read it five times.

Yeah, it was good to get in some non-Tamal time. But mostly Devane arrived early because she wanted to get in some extra practice time. She was a star already. No doubt. But that wasn't quite good enough. What she wanted to be was a superstar. She wanted to torch the stage at world. She wanted to blind every person in the audience to every dancer but Devane. If that took extra practice time, that was no problem. No one could accuse Divine Devane of being afraid of sweat.

"I see music videos. I see hip-hop instructional DVDs," said a man's voice. The words jerked Devane to a stop. It was like whoever was talking was speaking Devane's hopes and dreams out loud. *She* wanted a music video. *She* wanted to do some hip-hop classes on DVD! "I see the Hip Hop Kidz opening for the Peas and for Nas," the man's voice continued. Devane realized it was coming from Maddy's office. She took a cautious step closer. She had to hear every word.

"Well, it's certainly intriguing," Maddy said. "But I don't want to make any kind of decision until after the kids get back from the nationals."

"Come on, you know they're going to make it to world," the man said.

He and Devane really could share a brain. Of course the Hip Hop Kidz were going to win the nationals and go on to the World Hip-Hop Championship. Then win that, too!

"I hope so," Maddy answered.

"The offer I'm making is only for champions," the man told her.

"Even if they do win, I'm not sure all the kids are ready for what you're talking about. I need to think," Maddy told him.

"Definitely. You think. And we'll talk again in L.A.," the man answered. A second later, he strode out into the hall, almost running into Devane.

Slick, she thought. That word described him. From his slicked-back hair and his slick green-blue suit to the slick talk he'd been handing Maddy.

"I know you. You're Devane, I'm Rick Mars," Mr. Slick said. "You shine onstage. I saw you at the regionals."

Devane grinned. "We burned the place up that night."

Rick laughed. "You're not shy. And you're not modest. I like that." He gave her a quick wave as he headed off down the hall.

Devane stared after him. She had a feeling he was the kind of guy who could cut her five-year plan for world domination down to three. Maybe even two. She hurried to the empty practice room. Rick was going to be in L.A., and Devane was going to show him that she was up for videos, DVDs, and whatever else he needed a champion to take care of.

"So what am I supposed to wear, you think?" Emerson asked the girls in the locker room as they got ready for class.

"Have any of you been to a dance at Bellerman?"

Devane snorted as she sat down on one of the wooden benches and started untying her street shoes. "Girls from Overtown don't usually get invited to dances in that neighborhood. Don't you have to show an American Express black card before they'll even let you in?"

"Who would want to get in?" Chloe asked as she started her pre-class ritual of taking out all her earrings except one pair. A Gina rule. "No offense, Em. But whenever I see those private-school boys all dressed alike in their ties and blazers, it just gives me the creeps."

I'd probably give her the creeps in my uniform, too, Emerson thought. She didn't wear a tie. But a blazer was an optional part of her school dress code. That or an appropriate sweater over a white blouse.

"This from the girl who has a bracelet made of little skulls," Sophie joked.

"They aren't real," Chloe protested, then grinned. "Although it would be kind of cool if they were. But where would you get ones that small?"

"Come on. I need help here. This is my first date," Emerson confessed.

"Awww," Becca cooed, scooping her long red hair into a ponytail.

"That's so cool!" Sophie exclaimed.

Emerson was actually getting excited about the date.

Partially because it *was* her first date ever. But also because Wes was cute. And he would probably act a lot different when they were by themselves. It wasn't like she was the full-on Emerson that night at dinner, either. At the dance, she could be the Em she was with her friends. And she'd get to see what Wes was like with his friends, too.

"What kind of dance is it?" Sammi asked. "Sometimes a winter dance is more formal. But it seems a little early for that."

"I think his—" Emerson began, then stopped herself. She'd been about to say that she thought his mother would have told her mother if the dance was a semiformal or anything like that. "I think he would have told me that."

Sammi shook her head. "That's the kind of thing a lot of boys would totally *not* think to mention. Then you show up in a denim skirt while everyone else is dressed for the prom. You need to call up your boyfriend and ask him."

"He's not my boyfriend," Emerson protested.

But . . . it would be kind of fun to have a boyfriend. She was in seventh grade now. Other girls were starting to head into boyfriend territory. Em had been wondering when she would—if she would. If someone would ever like her like that.

Not that she was planning on blurting that out to everyone in the locker room. She'd save that for a Sophie-only conversation.

"He asked you to this dance," Becca said. "That means he probably wants to be your boyfriend."

Maybe Wes asked his mom to ask my mom to ask me, Emerson thought. *Maybe he really wants me to go to the dance with him.*

Maybe my first date is an actual, real date!

And knee in, knee out, look left, and hold. Sophie held the position, part of the frame of people around Fridge and M.J., who were taking on the final solo. At least today. Gina hadn't made a final decision about who would have the solos in the competition yet.

"Great work, everyone," Gina called out. "From here on out we're going to start spending the last ten minutes of class looking at tapes of the crews we'll be going up against at the nationals."

"And at world," M.J. and Devane added at the same time.

"And at world," Gina corrected herself with a smile. "Although I want you all to remember that just getting to the nationals is a huge accomplishment." She walked over to the TV and VCR she had set up next to the sound system. "The first group we're going to be looking at is the Hip Hop Shoowops."

"How many groups are competing against us?" Chloe

asked, rubbing a finger over all the empty holes in her left ear.

"There are thirty-two competing at the varsity level— that's age twelve to seventeen," Gina answered. She clicked on the TV and pushed PLAY on the VCR.

Sophie's eyes darted around the screen as she tried to decide where to look first. A guy in the front row slid a girl through his legs, spun around, and popped her into the air. Then he lowered her to the ground, both their bodies shivering like little earthquakes were running through them. On the left side of the stage, a girl had just rolled over a guy's back, her legs in a wide split.

"They use a lot of swing-dance moves in their routines," Gina commented. "A lot of hip-hop groups from Japan do, too. You'd think it would look kind of old-fashioned, but—"

"That lift was flippin' sweet," M.J. interrupted as one of the Shoowops rolled up onto her partner's shoulders, slid down his back, and landed on the floor in a crouch.

The mix of swing, hip-hop, and gymnastics made the crew's performance pop. The Hip Hop Kidz were going to have to bring it big time to beat them. "Where are the Shoowops from?" Sophie asked.

"They're the locals," Gina said. "Right from Los Angeles."

"Where do we get to stay in L.A.?" Max did a few monkey arms as she talked. She was always moving. Sophie would bet cash money she was a sleepwalker. There was no way Max could stay still for eight hours of ZZZs.

"Who cares about that?" Fridge broke in before Gina could reply. "What I want to know is, who are the judges?"

"Yeah, who is going—" Allan began.

"—to be judging us?" Adam finished for his twin.

Out of the corner of her eye, Sophie saw ill papi stiffen. She got it immediately. He was worried that his dad, J-Bang, was going to be a judge again, like he'd been for the regionals.

That's how ill papi had ended up on probation. He'd basically quit the group without telling anyone. He skipped out on the competition with no notice. Zero. Not even a phone call ten minutes before the Hip Hop Kidz were supposed to storm the stage.

Sophie had gone all Nancy Drew and figured out his deal. Even though ill papi talked all the time about his dad, who was an old-school hip-hop legend, and made it seem like J-Bang was teaching him moves and all, it turned out J-Bang had left ill papi and his mom when ill papi was a little kid. Ill papi had known the truth would come out at the competition because everyone would realize J-Bang had no idea who ill papi even was. So he'd stopped coming to class and pretty much disappeared—including leaving the whole crew hanging at the competition.

But Sophie had convinced him that he had to come back

to class, and ill papi ended up telling everyone the truth. He was a Hip Hop Kid again, but he was still on probation.

"Injuzi Hamilton, one of the stars of the Broadway show *Down Payment*, is a judge," Gina answered. Sophie held her breath as Gina continued. "Alicia Mendez—"

"She was the nice judge on *Celebrity Dance-Off*," Rachel jumped in.

Gina nodded. "And Extian. I guess no one needs me to explain who he is after the Grammys."

"He's my soon-to-be boyfriend, once I get to California," Becca joked, tossing her long red hair.

Sophie let out the breath she'd been holding. She could feel ill papi relax. It was like he'd been shooting out little needles of anxiety. And now all she was getting from him was waves of calm.

"J-Bang will be emceeing the national and world competitions." Gina glanced at ill papi as she made the announcement, and it seemed like everyone else in the room was suddenly looking at him, too. Sophie made sure to keep her eyes away. The last thing ills needed right now was to be stared at.

Gina clapped her hands. "That's it for today. Thanks, everybody!"

The second the last word left Gina's mouth, Rachel slipped on her iPod. Sophie shook her head. The girl could never wait to get back to her indie music.

Do I bring the dad thing up to ill papi? Sophie wondered as she headed for the door. *Or should I keep my mouth shut?*

Ill papi snagged Sophie by the arm and tugged her toward the soda machine at the opposite end of the hall from the locker rooms. "What am I supposed to do now?" he asked, making Sophie's decision for her. "I guess I could just skip the whole thing. It's not like I'm going to be dancing or anything. I'm still on probation."

"That doesn't mean you're not part of the group," Sophie told him. "And you're our alternate. We need you. If someone gets sick, or stubs a toe or something, and you're not there, we're dead in the water."

"A stubbed toe isn't going to keep anybody on our crew from taking the stage," ill papi said.

"It's not going to be like the regionals," Sophie promised him. "This time, everybody in the group knows the deal with you and J-Bang. And nobody else is going to care. You don't have to worry about keeping anything a secret."

"Yeah." Ill papi used his fingers to comb his dark hair away from his face. "But what if he recognizes me? I don't really want him trying to talk to me or anything. He hasn't bothered to see me since I was four. I don't want to have to deal with it just because we happen to end up in an auditorium together."

"Maybe he won't want to go there, either," Sophie

offered. "Maybe he's more freaked out than you. I mean, he's the one who left."

"Maybe. But . . ."

"Yeah, but maybe not," Sophie said, filling in the words her friend had left out. They were getting to be a little like the twins that way. "So what we need is a plan. And as you may have noticed when I wanted to get you back in the group, I am excellent with plans. I'm the master planner."

CHAPTER 3

"You want butter flavoring?" the girl behind the movie concession stand asked. She seemed way too irritated for someone who got paid to serve popcorn and soda. How hard could it be?

"My big brother always tells this story about how the first time I went to the movies, I thought they were asking if I wanted butter *or* flavoring, and I said I wanted cherry," Ky said.

"Aww." Sammi patted his arm.

"You want butter flavoring?" Irritated Girl snapped.

"You think it's being forced to wear the polyester uniform or inhaling all the fake butter fumes that's turned her into such a witch?" Sammi whispered to Ky.

Irritated Girl thrust the large popcorn into Ky's hands. "You're taking it without the butter. That's twelve seventy-five."

"I think we should get a discount since the theater's slogan is 'A fun place for film' and your attitude is not adding to our fun," Sammi said, pulling out her wallet.

"Wait. I'm paying for this," Ky protested.

"I asked you, so I'm paying," Sammi told him.

"But it's a date. A date means the guy pays," Ky told her.

"Step back, caveguy," Sammi joked. "Girls, they have jobs now. And their own money. Not that this money is technically mine. It's my parents'. But I have the same capacity to make bucks as you." She started to hand a twenty to the irritated one, but Ky grabbed her wrist.

"Come on. You got the tickets—but only because you ended up getting here first. I get to pay for this." He was starting to sound a little upset. Like it was actually a big deal one way or the other.

"Somebody pay right now," the girl behind the counter demanded.

Ky didn't let go of Sammi's wrist. But his grip was light. She could easily pull away. She shrugged. "If it means so much to you . . ."

Ky grinned as he handed over cash from his pocket to Irritated Girl. She shoved it in the cash register and slapped the change into his hand. "Thank you," Ky said, syrupy sweet.

"Let's get away before she zaps you with death rays from her eyes," Sammi suggested. They rushed away from the concession stand, laughing, and headed down to the theater showing the newest *Horror Movie* movie.

"I would have gone to see that chick flick. *It Girl* or whatever it's called," Ky said as they grabbed a couple seats near the front.

"*A Girl Thing*," Sammi corrected him. "And I didn't ask you to the movies to torture you. Anyway, I love the *Horror Movie* series. That part in the last one, where the man was trying to shove his second head back into his stomach before it could say anything to the girl, cracked me up."

"Me too." Ky stared straight ahead at the trivia question up on the movie screen. Just stared. Which was weird, because Ky usually liked to talk.

"I think the answer's Jennifer Garner," Sammi offered.

"Yeah, it definitely is," Ky said.

So he hadn't been staring at the screen trying to come up with the answer. Ky kept his eyes forward, even though the question hadn't changed. The silence felt like it was a physical force, pushing them apart.

Sammi knew she should say something, but she was too busy trying to figure out what kind of alien had taken over Ky's body.

"So, uh, what's your favorite subject in school?" Ky finally asked.

What's my favorite subject in school? Sammi silently repeated. She and Ky were way beyond that. They'd talked about all kinds of stuff, real stuff. Like her ill papi crush. And how he felt when he'd messed up his wrist and had to give up playing basketball, even though he was amazing at it.

"Basket weaving," Sammi joked.

"Uh-huh. Cool," Ky said.

He hadn't even heard what she'd said. "You excited about going to L.A.?" Sammi asked. It wasn't a brilliant question, either. But it was better than the favorite-subject one. And thinking about the trip and the competition might snap Ky out of whatever semi-coma he was in.

"Yeah. Yeah. Are you?" Ky asked.

"Absolutely," Sammi answered. "I've never been to L.A. I've never been anywhere in California." She reached into the popcorn bag and her fingers hit Ky's hand. It was wet and clammy with sweat.

Then Sammi got it. The weird silences. The not listening. The lame questions. The insistence on paying. The nervousness.

Being at the movie with her was a big deal to Ky. As in *big*.

He really liked her. *Liked* her liked her. Not that she didn't like him. She totally did. He was great. And she'd wanted to hang with him, because he was smart and cute and funny, and because he was a guy who wanted to hang with her, unlike ill papi.

But she hadn't known he liked her in a way that would make his hands sweat and cause him to lose the ability to speak and think.

He's acting the way I'd probably act if I ever ended up

going out with ill papi, Sammi realized. I'm *Ky's ill papi.*

Aw, that was so sweet.

"So, what's your favorite subject?" Wes asked Emerson, speaking loudly to be heard over the pulsing music.

Is this what they were going to talk about now? They'd already had a long conversation about what kind of soda to get. And they'd had a conversation with one of Wes's friends a while ago that was all "Where do you live?" and "What school do you go to?"

She'd been hoping she and Wes would both be able to act a little more normal by now. It was already more than an hour into the dance.

Maybe he's just really shy, she told herself. *Or nervous.*

She was nervous. Maybe it was a first-date thing. Was this Wes's first date, too? She wished she could ask him. But she wasn't anywhere close to feeling that comfortable.

"Definitely not French," she answered. "I am so bad at French. I even had to get a tutor this year. But I like history a lot, especially European history. It's like all these great stories—with actual queens, and kings, and betrayal, and secret love affairs—but they're actually true."

"Were your parents upset that you had to get a tutor?" Wes looked a little upset by the idea himself.

"Well, they definitely would have preferred that I

was naturally brilliant enough to have learned French in preschool," Emerson admitted. "But if I need a tutor to make the grades, they want me to have one." *Maybe I shouldn't have brought up the bad-in-French thing*, she thought.

"I actually did start learning French in preschool," Wes said. "My parents found a bilingual school, plus I had a nanny who spoke French to me all the time."

"Wow." That was all Emerson could think to say. Wes was way more perfect than she could ever hope to be. And it seemed like maybe he even liked being perfect. "Are you really as perfect as you sound?" she asked him. "Or is there actually something that you're not good at that I haven't figured out?"

"Um . . ." Wes stared up at the ceiling, thinking.

Please come up with something, Emerson silently begged. There was no way she could have a perfect person as a boyfriend.

"I'm not good at dancing. At least that kind." He jerked his chin toward the dance floor, where kids were freestyling it in all kinds of ways, only some of which could even really be called dancing. "My parents sent me to ballroom dance classes when one of my cousins was getting married. So I can do that."

Now I know why he's practically been glued to the wall all night, Emerson thought. *It's not because he's shy. Or because he doesn't want to be here. Or because he doesn't like me.*

She'd been trying to decide whether he liked her—even a little—since they'd arrived. She kept wondering if he was here because of his mother, or because he wanted to come to the dance, or because he wanted to come to the dance with *her.*

Emerson had also been trying to decide whether she liked Wes—even a little. Whether he was a guy she could imagine having as a boyfriend. Whether she even wanted one. Which she was pretty sure she did—if the boy was the right one.

She hadn't come to any conclusion. Wes was definitely still cute, with that strawberry-blond hair that had just a little curl in it. But . . . he wasn't that interesting to talk to. And she wasn't exactly having fun.

It could all just be first-date weirdness, she thought. *Even if it's not Wes's first date ever, it's his first date with me. And we hardly know each other.*

"Well, the kind of dancing everyone is doing here is a lot easier than ballroom," Emerson said. "There aren't any rules. You can do pretty much anything and it's okay."

Wes looked skeptical. Emerson decided to try and convince him. Maybe if they could just dance a little, the night would turn around and they'd have a good time.

Em had thought she'd feel like herself once she was out of sight of all the parents. But she didn't. She was analyzing practically everything she did or said, trying to decide if it was the right datelike behavior. Dancing would help. She usually didn't think about anything when she danced.

She glanced around the room. "Like that guy," she told Wes, nodding at a boy who was basically pumping his fist in the air while tapping one foot. "What he's doing is completely acceptable. So do you want to go out there and—" She pumped her fist in the air once.

"No, thanks," Wes said. "I don't think . . . it's not like I'll need to know how to dance like that."

But it's fun, Emerson wanted to tell him, but she didn't. She felt like she'd pushed him enough. "So . . . what's your favorite subject?" It was all she could think of to say.

Wes didn't seem to mind. He answered. They got another soda. They talked about his violin and her ballet, even though they'd covered both topics when he was over for dinner at her house.

Then it was over. And Emerson was more than ready to go home.

Your first date ever is supposed to be such a big deal, she thought. *So special. So amazing.*

This so wasn't.

"So, this was good," Wes said as they headed outside.

"Yes. Thank you for taking me," Emerson replied.

"We should do something else sometime."

"Really?" The word just sprang out of her mouth.

Wes stopped and looked at her. "Why do you sound so surprised?"

Emerson figured she might as well go for the truth. It was the end of the night. And she'd already blown it with that "Really?"

"I guess I just thought . . ." She shrugged. "I thought maybe you weren't having that much fun tonight. I thought maybe this whole thing was just something your parents— and mine, too—wanted, and maybe you didn't."

"It was my mom's idea," Wes confessed.

It wasn't a surprise. But it still hurt.

"But I thought you were cool that night at dinner," Wes continued.

"Really?" She couldn't believe she'd done the "Really?" blurt again.

"Yeah. You seemed kind of like me. Smart—like when you were talking about that painting. And you do ballet and I play the violin," Wes told her.

Used to do ballet, Emerson silently corrected him. But maybe he was right. Maybe they did have some stuff in common. Maybe after they knew each other a little better—

"We might end up at the same college, even," Wes went on, jerking Emerson away from her thoughts. "Your parents probably have the same list of schools that mine do. I'm already working with some to get my extra-curricular activities planned out. The violin's part of that."

Wes started to walk again, cutting across a stretch of perfect emerald green grass as they headed to the parking lot where they were getting picked up. "Anyway, so even though coming to the dance was my parents' idea, I was good with it. I mean, my parents like you. That's enough for me."

But it's not enough for me, Emerson thought. *Not nearly enough.*

"So did you come up with a plan?" ill papi asked Sophie when she plopped down next to him on the front steps of his apartment building on Saturday morning.

"Did I come up with a plan?" she scoffed. "Did I say I was going to come up with a plan?" She stared at him until he said yes.

"I'm going to need it louder than that," Sophie told him.

"Yes!" ill papi half-shouted. "So what is it?"

"Okay, I found out that right now, as we're sitting here, your dad is teaching a hip-hop workshop in Orlando that ends on Friday. My plan is that we figure out what hotel he's staying at, then you call him and ask to meet up with him."

"You were supposed to come up with a way for me to *not* have to deal with my dad," ill papi pointed out.

"I know. But I made a whatchamacallit, an executive

decision, and changed the plan," Sophie said. "See, you're going to have to deal with him at some point. Because the two of you are going to be in the same place at the same time. You can try and avoid him, but that's just one way of dealing. My plan is better. It's like if you know you have to go to the dentist. Wouldn't you rather just get it over with?"

"I guess," ill papi said slowly.

"Well, if you arrange a meeting with your dad now, you won't have a dentist appointment in L.A. You can just have fun. So what do you say?" Sophie asked.

She studied his face, trying to guess what he was thinking. He was either going to tell her to get off his stoop and never talk to him again, or they were going to start calling hotels in Orlando. *Come on, ills*, she silently coached. *Be brave like I know you can be.*

"I guess there are a couple things I wouldn't mind asking him," ill papi admitted. "And I wouldn't be wondering the whole time I'm in L.A. if he's going to try and talk to me or avoid me or what."

"Exactly," Sophie said. "You call him, that makes you the one in charge."

"So now all we have to do is find him. In Orlando. Not exactly a small town," Ill papi said.

"I went to the library and did a little research on one of the computers. I MapQuested the place where J-Bang's teaching the class, then I did a search for hotels right around there." Sophie pulled some folded sheets of paper out of her pocket and handed them over. "The circled ones are our targets."

Ill papi looked at the papers, then at Sophie, then back at the papers, then back at Sophie. "You really are the master planner."

"You don't lie, my friend." She felt like she'd swallowed a little piece of the sun and that it had lit up her insides. That's how good it was to have helped ill papi out. 'Cause she *liked* him. And it was even okay that he didn't *like* her back. 'Cause they were buds, and that was enough.

"My mom's at work, so we should make the calls now." Ill papi sprang to his feet and took the four steps to the main apartment door in two long strides. Then he turned back to face Sophie. "Except . . ."

She couldn't do the mind-reading thing this time. "Except?" she repeated.

"Except, what am I supposed to say when I do find him?" ill papi asked.

"What do you want to say?" Sophie responded as she joined him. "Haven't you ever imagined it? What you'd say if you ever did have the chance?"

Ill papi smiled, showing off his dimple. Sophie loved that dimple. "If I start describing the kinds of torture I came up for him when I was, like, ten, I'm pretty sure he'll hang up on me, then call the police." He opened the door and led the way inside.

"All righty, then. Maybe you should just keep it basic. Say that you're his son, and that you'd like to get together to talk to him. His dance workshop ends on Friday. Say you want to do it Saturday. A week from today," Sophie suggested as they started up the stairs to ill papi's apartment.

Ill papi unlocked his front door with a key attached to a long chain hooked to one of his belt loops. "What if he still hangs up? Or says that he wouldn't have left if he ever wanted to talk to me?" ill papi asked, looking forward and not at Sophie.

"Then . . . then . . ." Sophie hadn't thought about this possibility. Some master planner she was. "Then fine. Then you tell him—even if it means calling him back—that not speaking to him isn't a problem for you. Tell him that you're going to be at the nationals and probably at world, and you know he'll be there, too, and that you won't try to talk to him there, and he should do the same. Then there won't be any surprises for anyone."

"Yeah." Ill papi shoved open the door, ushered Sophie inside, then followed her. "That's the whole point of meeting with him, right? If he tells me on the phone he doesn't want to ever talk to me, that's even better than having to meet him in person. Taking the bus to Orlando or whatever."

"Uh-huh." Sophie nodded until she felt like a bobblehead dog in the back of a car window. But she didn't think the phone thing was better. And she didn't think ill papi did, either. What she thought was that it would really, really hurt.

Still, if that was J-Bang's 'tude, it would come out sooner or later. Better now, at home, with a friend nearby.

Ill papi grabbed the phone off the counter that divided the kitchen from the living room and plopped down on the couch. He glanced at the top sheet of Sophie's papers, dialed two numbers, then hung up. "So, I just say, 'Hi, this is ill papi'?" he asked Sophie as she sat down next to him. "No, wait. It's not like I was called that when I was four. So, it should be, 'Hi, this is Tim. This is your . . . son, Tim.'"

It sounded like ill papi had to swallow a large rock before he said the word *son*. "That part's good. Then what?" Sophie prompted.

"Uh, I wanted to know if you had time to meet up with me next Saturday. There are some things I want to talk to you about."

"Stellar," Sophie told him. She didn't want him to see her crossing her fingers for luck as he started to dial, so she crossed her toes instead. Her feet were starting to cramp by the time one of the hotels said they had a Kevin Quevas— aka J-Bang—registered.

Sophie leaned closer to ill papi as he said the lines he'd rehearsed. So close she could hear J-Bang's answer. "Uh, sure. Why not. Yeah, let's meet up."

CHAPTER 4

"So, tell us about the big date, Emerson," Becca said as the girls got dressed for class on Monday.

Sophie shot Emerson a sympathetic look. Emerson had already told Sophie everything. She'd called her up the second she got home.

"The outfit you guys said I should wear was perfect," Em answered.

Max hoisted herself on top of one of the rows of lockers and stretched out on her back. "That's not what we want to know."

"Was the band any good?" Rachel asked without taking off her iPod.

"That's not what we want to know, either," Devane said before Emerson could answer. "Give it up, girlfriend." She grinned at Emerson. "Was it a blast or a pass?"

"It was . . . nice," Emerson answered. Which is what she'd told her mother. "Actually, he was boring," she added. "And he basically said the reason he went with me was that his parents liked me."

"Yowch," Sammi said.

"Definite pass," Devane agreed.

"Well, it's not as if he didn't like me. His parents didn't *force* him to go or anything like that," Emerson explained.

"Still." Becca shook her head. "That is not the guy for you. Next! That's what I say."

"That's right," Devane said. "Next!"

Next. Like there was a whole line of guys waiting for Emerson. It wasn't like the dance was her first date because she'd turned down a bunch of other invitations. The boys at Emerson's school didn't seem to notice her.

Not in a mean way. It was always fine when Emerson was assigned to work in a group with guys. They talked to her . . . but it was like they didn't seem to notice her as a possible girlfriend. Emerson wondered if a boy ever would.

Sammi stopped for some water at the drinking fountain as she headed for the practice room. Suddenly, she felt two fingers run up her back. She snapped upright, coughing, the water she'd been trying to drink spurting out of her mouth.

"Whoa, sorry," Ky said as she spun around to face him. "I sometimes forget my power over women." He patted his pockets. "Nope, no Kleenex. Not a guy thing."

"It's okay," Sammi told him, starting to wipe the water

off with the back of her hand.

"No, wait, I got it." Ky grabbed the bottom of his T-shirt and used it to carefully wipe the water off her chin. "It's clean, I swear."

"Thanks," Sammi said. She smiled at him. How cute was that?

"Sure," Ky answered. He didn't step away. He was standing so close, just staring down at her.

"Doesn't look like Sammi is ready to say 'Next' to Ky," Sammi heard someone—she thought it was Becca—say.

Ky reached out to brush Sammi's hair away from her face.

"Do you think Gina is finally going to choose the solos today?" another voice asked.

Sammi jerked away. Ill papi. That was ill papi's voice.

"What's wrong?" Ky asked.

"Nothing. I, um—" *Think, think, think*, Sammi ordered herself. She couldn't tell the truth. There was no way she could tell Ky that she didn't want ill papi to see him touching her. Acting all boyfriendish. "I forgot something in the locker room. I just remembered. See you in there."

She took off down the hall. She thought she could feel Ky staring after her.

But she didn't look back.

Devane heard the beats of Black Ice's latest as she walked toward the mini-mart to buy herself a slushie on Friday afternoon. Loud beats. With the sounds of cheers and laughter mixed in. Could there be a block party happening?

She hadn't been to a block party in forever. Not since Gloria Neely moved away, she realized. Gloria loved to get up at parties, and even though she was only in elementary school when Devane knew her, she could always make her block stop what it was doing and rock.

And Devane was talking the whole block. All kinds of people. Toddlers who could hardly stay on their feet. Grannies sitting on stoops. Teenagers who normally acted too cool to hang with anybody but each other.

Devane grinned. A block party was what she needed. The newest moves weren't on MTV, or even something she could pick up in the Hip Hop Kidz Performance Group class. The street was where the truly killa moves were born.

Devane headed toward the music, wishing Gloria was with her. She hadn't thought about the girl in forever, but no one was more fun than Glow. Like in third grade, when she got really into ancient Egypt and came up with this game where she pretended that one of Tamal's stuffed alligators was the god Set, and she and Devane performed rituals for it. Devane didn't remember all the details, but she did remember her heart pounding when she got close to that goofy gator. Gloria could make anything drama-filled.

In a good way.

Devane turned the corner and it was like entering a different world. A world where people danced instead of walked. The whole street was moving. Everybody was dancing, not just a few b-boys and girls.

Like that guy over there, who had to be pushing forty. He was all up in his boxing—which was already a variation of tutting—doing things Devane hadn't quite seen before. Usually with boxing, a person just made squares or rectangles out of his or her arms. This guy was using his whole body, making shapes that looked like something out of Devane's geometry book with his arms and hands and fingers and legs and neck and even toes all at different angles.

Then he'd break down the shapes by turning his joints into hinges. He'd tap his elbow, and it was like that allowed his arm to start swinging. When his arm hit his knee, the bottom half of his leg started going. Devane watched as his leg moved up and down, getting higher with each arc until it got so high, the guy actually managed to tap his own chin. And that got the guy's neck hinge going. It was pretty freaky. Freaky cool.

The guy caught her watching him and smiled. He let his neck hinge back and forth, so it looked like he was nodding for her to come over. Why not? That was what she was here for. Devane approached him and faced off. Then she twisted her body into an angular shape at least as complicated as the old guy's.

She grinned as the man's elbow hinged back and forth. Eventually he let his arm hit her wrist. Devane let her wrist start hinging, like a door flopping back and forth in a breeze, like it wasn't even flesh. In a second, she'd let her wrist smack her waist. She knew she could do a smokin' waist hinge.

If this kind of styling wouldn't get her into one of the videos Mr. Rick Slick from Maddy's office wanted to make, then he didn't know jack. This was exactly what should be in the newest music video. It was exactly what people would want to learn on a hip-hop instructional DVD. The real down-and-dirty moves.

Devane just had to make sure Mr. Slick knew she was the Hip Hop Kid he was looking for. She knew everybody in the group would want to show him their stuff, and she'd even considered telling them all about Mr. Slick and what she'd overheard him talking about with Maddy.

'Cause Devane was all about being a team player now. She knew that hurting a teammate was only hurting the team. And hurting the team—especially during a competition—only ended up hurting yourself.

But not telling the team about Mr. Slick—that wouldn't exactly hurt them. It would just give her an edge, a little extra help getting in those videos Devane was pretty sure he'd been trying to talk Maddy into doing with the Kidz.

You could be a team player without telling everybody

absolutely everything. Nobody would ever have to know she'd overheard any of Maddy and Mr. Slick's convo. Devane started rocking back and forth from her waist, like a robo-girl. Yeah, Mr. Slick would *have* to want a move like this in one of his videos. And no one was going to do it better than Devane, once she got a little more practice in.

"Your father and I ran into Mr. and Mrs. Douglas at the charity auction for the Spinal Muscular Atrophy Foundation last night," Mrs. Lane told Emerson on Wednesday morning. "Mrs. Douglas said again what a good time Wes had with you at that dance."

Emerson sprinkled some sugar on her halved grapefruit, trying to decide how to answer. "That's nice," she finally said. "Did you and Dad have fun at the auction?"

"Your mother bought a chair that is too small for any human to sit on," Emerson's father answered as he poured himself a second cup of coffee. He always drank the first one in about three swallows.

"It's an antique. It's not for sitting," Emerson's mom said. "I thought it would be nice at the end of the hall. I can put that needlework pillow I just finished on it."

"Yeah, that's a good spot for something," Emerson agreed. "And it doesn't sound right for downstairs. Something old-fashioned wouldn't mix with all the modern furniture. What color is it?"

"Red," her father said.

"A kind of dusty maroon," her mother corrected. "Isn't there a dance coming up at your school this weekend, Em?" she asked, making a tire-screeching subject change.

Why couldn't she have kept talking about decorating? Emerson thought. Her mom loved to talk about what she had planned for the house. There was pretty much always one room that she was redoing. Emerson had figured that once her mother got going on the new chair, she'd keep on with the decorating talk through breakfast and forget all about Wes Douglas.

"I think there's a dance coming up, yes," Emerson answered. Actually, she was sure there was one on Friday. She spooned some grapefruit into her mouth.

"I was thinking it would be good manners if you asked Wes to go with you," Mrs. Lane said. "He invited you to his school, after all."

Emerson took her time chewing, but finally the piece of grapefruit was so mushy, she had to swallow. "Well . . . I wasn't planning to go to the dance at all," she explained. Which was true. "It's the last weekend before I leave for L.A., and I need to do a bunch of work on the assignments I got for the time I'll be gone." Which was also true.

But there was something else that was true: Emerson just didn't want to have to get through another night with

Wes. Another night that would feel like a date—but a date with someone who had no interest in the real Emerson.

"Well, there will be another dance after you get back," her mother said, exchanging a look with Emerson's dad. The kind that represented an entire conversation. "You'll have a lot more free time then."

Emerson nodded. She'd have a lot more free time, because she wouldn't be a Hip Hop Kid anymore. Her parents were allowing her to fulfill her obligation to the team by participating in the national championship—and world, if the group got that far.

But that was it. As soon as Emerson flew back from California and stepped off the plane in Florida, there would be no more hip-hop for her. Just dances with Wes and whatever else her parents came up for her to do.

No more fun.

Ever.

Sophie and ill papi sat side by side in a back booth of an Orlando Denny's. That way J-Bang could sit across from them when he got there. *If* he got there. He was already— Soph snuck a glance at her watch—eleven minutes late. *He better show, or I'm going to track him down and find a way to inflict some serious pain on him*, she thought.

She and ill papi had come by bus—and their seats had

been way too close to the smelly bathroom—from almost 235 miles away. J-Bang was supposedly coming from just a few blocks. If anybody had an excuse for lateness, it was them. But they'd been forty-two minutes early. Sophie'd had so many glasses of iced tea, she felt like she was going to burst. But there was no way she was going to risk a bathroom run and leave ill papi alone at what could be the critical moment.

Ill papi drained his soda and dumped some ice into his mouth. "I guess he won't recognize me," he said as he chomped. The sound of teeth on ice cubes gave Sophie goose bumps. Or maybe it was the idea of a father not recognizing his own kid.

"Well, we'll recognize him," she answered. "He's J-Bang. Everybody knows what he looks like."

Ill papi nodded as he swallowed his ice. "So what time is it now?"

"It's only a few minutes after eleven," Sophie said, without looking at her watch. "He's probably walking down the block as we speak." *Let it be true*, she silently pleaded. *Don't let ill papi's dad be a jerk. A bigger jerk than he already is by taking off on ill papi.*

Crunch. Crunch. Crunch. Ill papi got started on a new batch of ice cubes. Sophie scanned the restaurant. Their waitress was heading toward them. The look on her face made Sophie think that they weren't going to get away with more drink refills. Sophie's bladder made her think that it wasn't going to let her get away with more refills, either. Maybe they could order some toast or something, then get more when J-Bang got there.

Because he was getting there. Even though he was now—she took another sneak look at her watch—fifteen minutes late. Which somehow felt a lot longer than eleven.

"You kids are going to have to order something or give up that booth," their waitress said as she reached their table.

Knew it, Sophie thought. But she and ills couldn't order something big, because they had to have enough money to order something when J-Bang arrived. Plus money for the bus ride home. Maybe J-Bang would treat. Most dads would treat. Sophie's dad definitely would. But who knew about J-Bang?

"Could we split an order of toast?" Sophie asked.

"I suppose. But you'll need to eat it quick. This booth is—"

"That's him," ill papi said, interrupting her.

Sophie followed his gaze. Yep, that was J-Bang. And he was waving—at her. She'd forgotten he would recognize her from that time she talked to him at the regionals. That time she found out he had no idea that his son even used the name ill papi, never mind where ill papi actually was that night.

"That man's joining us," Sophie told the waitress. "Just

give us a second and we'll all order. Not just toast, okay?"

The waitress gave a little grunt and backed off. Then J-Bang slid into the seat across from Sophie and ill papi. He didn't try to reach over and give ills a half-hug or anything. Instead J-Bang did that thing where you stare at someone, but try not to look like you're staring. Ill papi didn't look at J-Bang at all. He just stared at the menu, even though he and Sophie pretty much had it memorized after being in the place for almost an hour.

"So, so, I'm glad you called, Tim," he said. "Uh, congratulations on going to the nationals. That's something I didn't do until I was twenty. And you're what? In the seventh grade?"

"Ninth," ill papi corrected.

"We're all really psyched," Sophie said to keep the conversation going. She figured spending some time on the light stuff would give ill papi and J-Bang a little time to get used to each other. That would be good before they moved on to the heavy stuff—the why-you-walked-out stuff. "We're hoping we get to go on to the World Hip-Hop Championship. You know how it happens right after the nationals. Did you get to world when you competed?"

"First time, no. Second and third time, yes," J-Bang told her.

Ill papi didn't say anything. *We should have rehearsed some of this conversation, too*, Sophie realized. *The way we rehearsed what he should say on the phone.*

"So, any tips for us?" She hoped if she asked enough questions, ill papi would start joining in.

"Have fun. It shows when you do. The judges can see it," J-Bang said, speaking directly to ill papi, who was still reading the menu. Rereading it.

"How did you get into hip-hop, anyway?" ill papi asked, without raising his eyes.

Sophie felt like jumping up and leading the rest of the restaurant in a cheer. Instead she smiled at both of them and tried not to think about how badly she had to pee.

"I can't even think of a time I wasn't into it. It was always just something I did," J-Bang began. The waitress interrupted to take their orders, and seemed satisfied by the amount of food. "Not in classes. Or in competitions. Just for myself. Hangin' with my friends. At least at first," J-Bang concluded. "How about you, Tim?"

"Ill papi," ill papi corrected.

"Ill papi," J-Bang repeated.

"Mom—" He stopped short, like he'd said something he shouldn't, then went on. "Mom's friends with the woman who runs the Hip Hop Kidz office. She told Mom she thought I'd like the classes, so Mom signed me up. That was a few years ago. She wanted me to have something to do to keep me busy after school, before she got home from work."

"Cool." J-Bang stood up. "Be right back. Just need to

use the facilities."

Sophie did, too. But she needed the alone time with ill papi more. "Okay," she said quietly. "I think when he gets back, you're ready to move on to the bigger stuff."

Ill papi raised his eyebrows, like he had no idea what she was talking about.

"You have your dad sitting right in front of you," Sophie explained. "Don't you want to talk to him about something real? You don't know when you're going to get another chance. Ask him everything you want to ask him. I can give you some privacy if you want."

"No," ill papi blurted out. "No, I want you to stay."

"Sure. Absolutely," Sophie promised. "I see him. He's coming back."

A moment later, J-Bang was again sitting across from them.

"So, there's something I want to ask you," J-Bang told ill papi before he could speak. "I was really happy you called, and I thought maybe we could go get you a cell phone, so we could talk more often. How would that be?"

This is so great! Sophie thought, her eyes darting from J-Bang to ill papi. *Now ills will be able to have lots of conversations with his pops.*

"I wanted to ask you something, too," ill papi replied, ignoring J-Bang's question. "Why'd you take off?" Ill papi's eyes glistened. "And why'd you act like I didn't even exist after you did?"

"That was wrong." J-Bang's eyes were wet, too. "All I can say is that I wasn't thinking of you right then, which was very wrong. I couldn't deal with your mother. At all. Not even to get to you. I just couldn't deal."

Ill papi stood up. "Let's go, Sophie."

"Wait," J-Bang protested. "I want things to change. I messed up. I—"

Ill papi was halfway across the restaurant. Sophie hurried after him.

When she'd come up with her master plan, she hadn't planned on this.

CHAPTER 5

Devane's stomach dropped into her lap as the plane rose off the runway on Tuesday morning. She pressed her forehead against the glass of the window and watched as the world got small. Cars became toys. Swimming pools turned into little stamps of sparkling turquoise. She tried to figure out where Overtown was. She bet even her part of the city looked cute from the air. Everything looked cuter—and cleaner—from up here.

"Have you guys ever been on a plane before?" Max asked, fiddling with the little knob overhead that controlled the airflow. She'd gotten stuck in the middle seat because she was the smallest kid in the group. Devane thought that Max should have been given the aisle. She was probably going to end up climbing over Fridge a zillion times. The girl just could not sit still.

"I haven't," Devane answered, turning toward Max. And somehow she'd expected it to be a little more . . . more. The seats weren't that much different than bus seats. And the seat belts were just like car seat belts, even though the flight attendant had demonstrated how to use them like they were something different. Still, being up in the air? That was just . . . thirty-one flavors of good.

"I went to visit my grandparents in New York once," Fridge said.

"I went to D.C. once. And to Indiana once," Max told them.

"Ever gone first class?" Devane asked, staring up at the curtain that separated the privileged from the regular people. Not that she was regular, but she was in the regular-people section.

"Yeah, right," Fridge answered.

"Even if we win world, we don't get to fly first class." Max grabbed the magazine from the seat pocket in front of her and started flipping through it.

Maybe not, Devane thought. *But if we win world and we do some videos, I bet we could go first class all the way. And that would be so Devane.*

Aside from what Maddy had said, if Mr. Slick did get to make videos like he wanted to, not everyone in the group would be in them. Maddy didn't think everyone was ready. But did that mean dancing ready? Or something else?

Devane kind of wished she could ask Max and Fridge what they thought. But she'd already decided she couldn't talk about Mr. Slick with the others. If only some of the Kidz were going to be able to do the music videos and instructional DVDs, that meant Max and Fridge—and everyone else in the group—were the competition. And Devane just didn't believe in sharing info with the competition.

"Anything to drink?" one of the flight attendants asked, pulling Devane out of her thoughts.

"Coke, please," Devane said. A moment later she had a cup of ice, a can of soda, and a mini bag of pretzels on the foldout tray in front of her. She carefully slid the pretzels into her purse.

"If you're not eating those, Fridge wants." He reached across Max and wiggled his fingers.

"Fridge doesn't get." Devane gave his hand a light slap. "These are going home to my little brother, Tamal. He's all excited about trying airplane food." She took a sip of her Coke, the carbonation tickling her nose. "I think when I'm a megastar, I'll buy him a plane. And a pilot. I hardly trust Tamal to steer a skateboard. Forget about something that travels thirty thousand feet in the air."

"You think big," Fridge said.

"She didn't get the nickname Diva for nothing," Max told him.

Devane didn't mind being called Diva. And it was true she had big plans—for herself, for her mom, even for Tamal.

If she had to practice till there was no sweat left in her body, plan till her brain ached, and keep a few secrets—even from her friends and teammates—that's just the way it had to be.

Emerson was surrounded by her teammates, who were also her friends. She was sitting right next to her best friend, Sophie. But she felt . . . lonely. Like they were all out of her life already.

Sure, Emerson could still see people from Hip Hop Kidz after they got back from California. Just because she had to quit the group didn't mean her parents were banning her from all kinds of communication. But they were going to want her to start taking ballet again. And Sophie and all the others would be taking their own classes and performing.

It would be a lot different than knowing she'd see them all every week, at the very least. And more when they had a show coming up. A salty lump began to form in Emerson's throat, and she swallowed hard to force it down.

You haven't quit the group yet, she told herself. *You're here right now. So enjoy it.*

But it was a hard order to follow.

Ill papi stared out the window of the plane. All Sophie could see was the back of his head. But she could still tell he was worried, and sad, and kind of mad, too. Which meant he was thinking about his dad.

She glanced over at Emerson, who was sitting on her other side. Em was staring straight ahead, her blue eyes blank. She was clearly deep in thought, and whatever she was thinking about wasn't all that happy, either.

They were on their way to L.A. They were going to compete in the nationals. Well, ill papi wasn't because of the probation, which sucked, but he was still with them. This was no time to be blue!

Sophie picked up the phone on the back of the seat in front of her. "Hello, I'd like to rent a pizza."

Emerson giggled.

That was better. Sophie kept on going. "But I need to know if it's organically grown."

"You're whack," ill papi said, turning away from the window.

Sophie smiled. Ill papi liked it when she was whack. He always smiled when he said it.

"Because I heard in L.A., people are mean to you if you eat food that isn't organic," she continued. "So are the pizzas grown locally or what?" She put the phone down. "They hung up on me," she told ill papi and Emerson.

Ill papi laughed. "You're whack," he said again.

"So whack," Emerson agreed, bumping shoulders with Sophie.

"Well, I hear there are some very nice, very relaxing

mental institutions in L.A.," Sophie answered. "I don't think they call them that. They might call them spas or something. So when we land, you two can check me into one. I expect to have a room next to someone with at least one Grammy or Oscar. An Emmy is acceptable, I guess. But not if it's a daytime one."

All three of them cracked up.

Sammi heard ill papi laugh. Again.

She glanced across the aisle at him. A glance that kind of turned into a look. A look/stare. It was just that he was so cute when he laughed with that dimple of his coming and going. Why was it Sophie who could always get him to crack up?

"There's this hot dog place in L.A. called Pink's," Ky told Sammi. "People supposedly line up to get the dogs there— line up down the block. I'm definitely going to find a way to check it out. Any hot dog that good, I'm getting down my throat. You want to go with me?"

Ky tapped Sammi's arm. "Blink once for yes. Twice for no."

Oops. Sammi had sort of zoned out around the part where Ky was talking about people waiting in line. Was the once for yes/twice for no question still about the hot dog place, or something else? She decided it would be stupid to answer if she really didn't know what he'd asked. "Sorry. What?"

"Never mind." Ky turned toward the window.

Sammi looked over at M.J. to see if he could fill her in, but M.J. was asleep, a single shining strand of drool running down his chin.

"Aw, look at sweet baby M.J.," Sammi whispered to Ky. He hesitated, then leaned across Sammi to get a look. "Think we should wipe it off for him?" she asked.

"I think we should take a picture. If he ever becomes one of the kings of hip-hop, we could sell it for big money," Ky replied.

"So, what were you asking before?" Sammi tried again. "Sorry I zonked. There's just so much going on in my head with the competition and going to California and everything." *Including ill papi sitting right across the aisle*, she silently added.

"No big. I wanted to know if you wanted to hit that Pink's place with me. See what makes their dogs so special," Ky said.

"Sure, I'll go. But I'll have to stick with fries or something. I'm a vegetarian." Sammi ate one of the pretzels from her little bag, then shook the bag in Ky's direction. He'd already Hoovered his.

"I can't believe I didn't remember that!" Ky exclaimed.

"Well, yeah, I do expect everyone I know to remember

every detail about me. Birthday, favorite foods, favorite color, favorite animal, that kind of thing. I think I'm going to have to make you take a test later," Sammi teased as she wondered what ill papi's favorite color was. She bet Sophie knew.

She took a fast look at ill papi. His favorite color should be maybe a burnt orange. It would look really good against his golden brown skin.

"Deal," Ky agreed. "But you have to help me study. Right now." He studied her for a moment. "So, what's your favorite nonmeat food?"

"Hmm, I'd have to say . . ."

Ill papi laughed. Probably at something Sophie said.

Sammi glanced over. A glance that turned into a look-slash-stare again. It was hard to just take a peek at ill papi.

"Don't you have any self-respect?" Ky demanded.

Sammi jerked her head toward him. "What?" she cried.

"The guy's not into you. It's obvious. Are you going to keep panting after him or what?" Ky asked, his eyes locked on hers.

You don't want to be with a guy who doesn't want to be with you, a little voice in Sammi's head said. *'Cause Ky's right. That's just pathetic.*

"No," Sammi told Ky, holding his gaze. "No, I'm not doing that. I want to hang out with a guy who wants to hang with me."

Ky smiled. "Good."

CHAPTER 6

"This place looks so familiar," Becca said as she climbed out of the airport shuttle van behind Devane.

Devane glanced from the small motel office to the two long buildings that formed an L around the smallish pool. "The building doesn't. But the pool does," Devane agreed. It was kidney shaped, with a mosaic of small black and white tiles around the edge. The umbrellas of the small tables dotted around the pool were either black or white or black-and-white striped.

"Picture a grizzly bear standing on the diving board, with a man in a tux serving him a—" the twenty-something guy helping them with their luggage began.

"It's the pool from the Get2It video," Devane and Becca cried together.

"Yep," the guy answered as he unloaded another suitcase from the van. "They filmed it here. And that place on the corner?" He nodded toward a neon sign that read *Meaty Meat Burgers.* "That's—"

"From the Sindy CD cover," Devane and Becca again said at the same time.

How much was Devane loving the flava of this spot? So very much.

"Would you two move so—" Adam began.

"—the rest of us can get off the van?" Allan finished for his brother.

Devane moved forward a few steps, checking out the pool again. She was definitely going to get someone to take a snap of her on the diving board. And in front of Meaty Meat Burgers. She had a shirt that was almost like the one Sindy had on for that CD, and she knew she could definitely serve up the Sindy attitude.

Devane decided she wanted a whole photo album filled with pictures of herself in scenes from famous videos and movies. "Is there anything else that was filmed at the motel? Or any other CD covers shot here?"

"Not right here," the guy answered. "But the screenplay for the first *Educator* movie was written in room 304. The woman who wrote it stayed in there for three weeks. She got every meal delivered from Meaty's. When she came out, it was done."

"Cool," M.J. said, joining the group. "I love those movies."

"Okay, guys, we've got you checked in," Gina said as she and Randall, who taught the hip-hop basics class and was one of the trip chaperones, headed toward them. "All of us are on the second floor." She tossed a key to Devane. "You, Max, Rachel, and Becca will be in 207. Head on up. Randall and I will get the luggage sorted out."

"Remember that number—207," Devane told the guy who was still unloading their luggage. "Someday you'll be telling people some of the hip-hop world champions stayed there!"

"I understand it takes the rest of you a little more time to look fabulous," Devane teased as she stepped into the motel room that Sammi, Sophie, Emerson, and Chloe were sharing. "But there are limits. The party is waiting."

"And we're just waiting for Soph," Sammi answered. "Who has tried on every piece of clothing she brought."

"I think she was even considering whipping up something from the shower curtain and my skull bracelet, *Project Runway*–style," Chloe added, with a grin.

"Don't forget the banana-peel trim," Sophie answered. She could feel her face turning red. *Get a grip. Nobody knows why you were trying on all the clothes in the known world*, she told herself. *Nobody has a clue you wanted to find an outfit ill papi would like.*

Which was dumb on so many levels. Level one: Sophie didn't think ill papi noticed what she wore. At all. Ever. Level two: Even if he did notice, it wouldn't matter, because ill papi wouldn't *like* like her due to what she was wearing. He didn't want to *like* like any girl. Level three: Even if ill papi didn't have a rule against the *like* like, there was almost zero chance he would *like* like Sophie. He was a ninth-grader, she was a sixth-grader. He was gorgeous, she was chunky-cute. He was . . . he was *ill papi*, the guy every girl at Hip Hop Kidz wanted. She was Sophie, the girl every guy she met wanted to be "just friends" with.

But even with the extreme-dumb factor, Sophie wanted to look as good as possible. "Is this okay?" she asked Sammi. Sammi had been voted Most Fashion Forward last year, when she was in the eighth grade. Sophie could totally trust her opinion on clothes and hair and all that.

"Love it," Sammi said.

"You just need earrings." Chloe pulled off one of her five pairs and handed them to Sophie.

"I feel sorry for the other crews at this welcome party," Devane said. "I mean, look at us. We scream 'champions.' The other teams are going to be so depressed, they're going to feel like leaving before the competition even starts."

"Except did you see M.J.?" Emerson asked. "I ran into him at the ice machine, and he's wearing his lucky socks."

"With the plaid and the orange?" Sophie rolled her eyes.

"And the smell," Devane reminded everyone. "You

know he hasn't washed those things since he got into the Performance Group a year and a half ago."

"At least he always wears that thin pair of socks underneath the lucky pair," Emerson said.

"Yeah, or the lucky socks would be very unlucky," Sophie added. "At least one of M.J.'s feet would have fallen off by now."

"Doesn't he realize the party is at a swanky beach house?" Sammi asked. "We're not going to be hanging at the pizza place next to Hip Hop Kidz. And those socks aren't even nice enough *there*."

"Well, M.J.'s cute. Maybe no one will look at his feet," Emerson offered.

"Yeah. We do have some cuties. Let's just make ill papi walk in first," Sammi suggested. "Then no one will notice anybody's socks. The girls will all be staring at ills. And guys never notice socks, anyway."

"Especially not with Soph in the house," Chloe added. "With my earrings, we're talking hot-hot-hot."

Will ill papi think so? Sophie couldn't stop the dumb-dumb-dumb thought from flashing through her head.

*This place would hold about—*Devane attempted a fast head count, then gave up. Forget the whole place. This living room, or great room, she guessed you were supposed to call it, would hold her family's apartment at least four times over. Maybe even five.

I gotta get me one of these places, Devane thought as she stared out the floor-to-ceiling windows at the lagoonlike pool outside. A waterfall splashed into a hot tub, which was as big as some pools back home in Florida. And it wasn't like Flash, the kid from the Hip Hop Shoowop crew who was hosting the party, and his family really even needed a pool. The ocean was practically at their back door. If someone walked around the pool and past the changing cabanas—stocked with tons of swimsuits—they'd end up at a long set of artfully weathered steps leading right down to the sand.

Devane took a sip of her Arnold Palmer. She'd ordered it from one of the bartenders scattered all over the place because she liked the upscale sound of the name, and it turned out that the tangy mix of iced tea and lemonade was her new favorite flava. Why wouldn't it be? Everything at this house was her new favorite, from the almond soap in the bathroom to the stained-glass tabletops on the patio.

Then Devane reminded herself that Mr. Slick had told Maddy he'd see her in L.A. Which meant that there was a good chance Devane could orchestrate a run-in to remind him that she was perfection and that he shouldn't even think of making a video or a DVD without her front and center. That would be the next step to Devane starring in her own music videos, acting, choreographing, producing, directing—all the things she knew she was born for. All the things that would get her a house, pool, and private slice of beach of her very own.

But Mr. Slick wouldn't be interested in any of the Hip Hop Kidz unless they turned out to be champions. Devane decided the best way to make that happen was to start checking out the competition. Kids from all the crews who would be competing against her crew were here tonight. They weren't doing their routines or anything. But they were dancing. Showing off some. And maybe revealing some weak spots.

Let's just see what we can see, Devane thought. She decided to try the beach first. There was a live band down there, and a lot of people were dancing around the bonfires. Although almost as many were upstairs: The DJ there was fierce, and the floor was perfect for slides and eggbeaters and every other move that required a smooth, hard surface. *I'll check out the dancing up there later,* she promised herself as she slipped outside into the cool night air. The temperature dropped a lot more at night out here than it did in Florida. A desert thing, the twins had explained on the van ride over from the motel.

"Hey, Dev, come on in," Fridge called from the center of the pool, where he was floating on a lounge chair.

"I'm heading to the beach," she called back. The two-day-long competition started on Thursday, and the Hip Hop

Kidz were up on Friday. They were going to be hitting the stage in almost no time. But Fridge had no problem getting lazy. Was she the only one who had thought to check out the competition?

Seemed that way. Becca was in the hot tub, letting the waterfall whoosh down over her long red hair while turning into a human prune. Max looked ready to attempt a cannonball that would sink Fridge—lounge chair and all. Devane bet the rest of the group members were all about having fun wherever they were, too.

Not that Devane didn't like fun. She just didn't let it rule her. She couldn't if she was going to be able to stick to the world-domination plan.

She started down the steps, then paused. *Now, who is looking especially like a world conqueror?* she thought as she scanned the crowd from above.

Hmm. There were some worthy dancers. A couple even Hip Hop Kidz–worthy. But there was only one girl who was Devane-worthy: That girl working a wave, her body flexing and relaxing in a way that made it appear like liquid. Devane hurried down the rest of the steps to get a better look, and the girl jerked to a stop and squealed. "Dee-Vee?"

No one had called Devane that in years. Who was this chick? Freckles. Arms and legs that seemed just a little too long. Blond hair that kept trying to go rasta. "Glow?" Devane exclaimed.

"Of course it's me!" Gloria Neely told her. "It hasn't been that long, girlfriend."

"Fourth grade. I'm in seventh now. That's three years since you moved away on me." Devane held up three fingers for emphasis.

"It would take a lot longer than that for me to forget you," Gloria insisted. "I can't believe you're here, though. What are you doing here?"

"I'm here to rock the nationals with my crew," Devane answered.

"You're one of those Florida Hip Hop Kidz! Omigod! I'm a Hip Hop Shoowop!" Gloria did a sped-up version of the wave.

"So we'll be doing battle." Devane gave her a mock scowl. Well, it was ninety-percent mock.

"Just like on those street dance parties we used to get together," Gloria agreed. "It's going to be so much fun."

Fun. Hmm. Her friend might be a Devane-worthy dancer. But she wasn't a Devane-worthy competitor. No one who really wanted to win would think of a competition as *fun.* A competition was a flat-out battle—to the death.

"You're Emerson Lane, right?" a tall, tan boy with sun-streaked brown hair and green eyes asked as Emerson stepped out of one of the cabanas in a Stella McCartney bathing suit she'd found.

"Um, yes." Was she supposed to know who the guy was? She'd definitely remember if she'd met him before.

"I'm Flash," he told her. "Or, to introduce myself the proper way, at least according to my parents, I'm Charles Harper. And it's a pleasure to meet you."

"Oh, you're the one giving the party!" Emerson exclaimed. "That's so cool of you—and your parents. I still don't get how you know my name, though."

"The Shoowops watched a tape of your crew to suss out who we'd be competing against. I asked who you were because I thought that strobing pirouette move you do is killer. You have to have taken ballet, too, am I right?" Flash asked.

"So much ballet. Practically since I could walk," Emerson answered. "We watched tapes of you guys, too. You're the one who does that over-the-back move with your partner, right?" The image of Flash's swing-infused hip-hop move came back to her in a rush. "Did you guys take separate swing-dance lessons or did you learn the moves during your regular class?"

"We did this weeklong intensive seminar during spring break with this couple who had won a bunch of awards for swing dancing. We rehearsed it vanilla for a while after that, then we started mixing it up with hip-hop," Flash explained.

Here I am, having a regular conversation with a boy, Emerson thought. After going to the dance with Wes, she wasn't sure that would even be possible. She thought every boy-encounter that wasn't absolutely, completely friend-only might be awkward and awful.

Although maybe this encounter was all-friend? Only something about the way Flash had smiled when he'd first come up to her—and he had come looking for *her*—made her think maybe not. At least not totally.

"Charles," a blond woman in a lilac tank-dress called as she headed toward them. "Please remember that this is your party. That means that you can't spend all your time talking to one person, no matter how pretty she is." The woman gave Emerson a wink. "You need to make sure your guests have everything they need." With a little wave, she disappeared inside.

"That was my mother. Being a good host is very important to her," Flash, aka Charles, explained.

"Your mom's just like my mom," Emerson said. "Except, not. Because your mom is clearly okay with you dancing hip-hop. I mean, she let you have the whole welcome party for all the crews competing at the varsity level here. My mom thinks I need an exorcism because I'm into hip-hop."

"But she let you come out here," Flash commented. "Or did you stow away in somebody's luggage or something?"

"Uhhh . . . long story," Emerson told him.

"So give me the *Soup* version."

Emerson shook her head. "Is that California speak, or—"

"No, it's this TV show where they do clips from other TV shows," Flash explained.

"So, the short version?"

Flash nodded.

"My parents were okay with me taking a few hip-hop classes as, you know, a summer activity. But that's it. When school started, they expected me to quit. They thought I only had time for one dance class, and that had to be ballet. My mom is on the arts council and having a daughter who does ballet and who's cast in the *Nutcracker* is very important—especially the part where the daughter and the mom on the council get their picture in the paper with the daughter in her *Nutcracker* costume—year after year. And . . . I guess this is turning out not to be the short version."

"Well, now I gotta hear the rest," Flash said. "Obviously, hip-hop didn't turn out to be just a summer thing, because you're here and it's not summer."

"Right." Emerson sucked in a long breath and continued. "See, I lied to my parents, went to hip-hop class instead of ballet. Then they found out. I had to quit hip-hop and basically live in my room without the phone or computer or anything that makes life worth living. The only reason I'm here is that my teammates convinced my parents it wasn't fair to the team if I didn't come for the nationals, and world if we get that far, since I'd been rehearsing as part of the group. But I have to quit again as soon as I get home."

"Whoa. That sucks," Flash said. "Can't you work out a deal, like I do with my parents? Basically, I do everything they want—get good grades, act like the perfect son in front of their friends, take clarinet lessons, all that. And as a reward, I get to do hip-hop."

"I guess I'm just not good enough to deserve a reward," Emerson admitted. "I'm bad at French."

Flash pressed his hands over his mouth in pretend horror.

"And I really don't have enough time to study and get tutored in French if I do hip-hop and ballet," she went on.

"And the ballet is non-negotiable?" Flash asked. "I'm big on negotiations."

"Completely non-negotiable," Emerson said. "Besides, I don't think my parents would ever agree to negotiate with a liar and a sneak."

"Yeah, I can see that you're a bad seed. I should probably stay far away from you," Flash joked. "We definitely shouldn't be seen dancing together." He held out his hand.

"But you're supposed to be mingling," Emerson reminded him.

"We'll go down to the beach. That way it will look like I've mingled. And if you see anyone about to pass out from hunger, point them out to me and I'll make like a host." Flash wiggled his fingers and this time Emerson took his hand.

As in, she was holding a boy's hand. A boy who actually seemed to get her. And didn't even know if his parents liked her or not.

"Everybody looks pretty happy," she observed. All Emerson saw were smiling, laughing people as they walked around the pool and over to the steps leading to the beach.

"I know. I don't get why my mom can't see that. She worries way too much. She's hired a million people to serve drinks and food and to clean up and everything, but somehow she can never relax."

"Just like my mom," Emerson said. "She has to stay in bed for about half a day after a party. And not because she's had too much fun—because she got too stressed out."

"I don't ever want to be like that," Flash told her as they hit the beach. "I'd rather have a tiny little hut and invite one person over at a time, if that's what it took."

Emerson laughed. "A hut. I like that. You could never get all obsessed about how to decorate a hut. Or what people think of the sand in front of your hut."

Flash boogied over toward the closest bonfire, pulling Emerson with him. The band was playing "Hey Ya!," a song that always made her want to dance, and they moved together like they had one brain. One brain with one body. She'd never felt that way before.

"Hey, you two! Don't forget you're competing!" a girl

with almost-dreads called to them.

"Not just competing," Devane called from beside the girl. "Enemies. Mortal enemies!" She and the girl both laughed.

"Have you met Devane?" Emerson asked Flash. "Devane, this is Flash Harper, our host. Flash, this is Devane. She's in Hip Hop Kidz, too."

"Nice intro," Flash joked. "You must have gone to charm school." He nodded toward the girl with Devane. "That's Gloria Neely. She's in the Shoowops with me."

"Devane and I have known each other since kindergarten. We grew up around the block from each other until I moved here in fourth grade," Gloria said.

"And you're telling *us* to remember we're enemies?" Flash asked them. "You should be telling each other that. Emerson and I just met. You two have known each other forever."

"So we all have to accept that we can't trust one another. And that we'd all kill even our best friend to win. Other than that, we can hang and become BFFs," Gloria joked.

Emerson laughed. But it was obvious Gloria was only half-kidding.

CHAPTER 7

Even though Sammi wasn't looking for ill papi—because she was dancing with Ky and it would be so not right to be looking for ill papi at the same time—she somehow knew where he was. He was over near the DJ with her sister. It was like she could sense him with her skin or something.

"It would be kind of freaky to have this room in your house and walk into it when it was empty," Ky said as they grooved to the music.

"Why? I think it would be kinda cool," Sammi told him. Oops. That last turn she'd made had left her with a direct view of ills. She forced herself to look straight into Ky's face. She wasn't going to let him catch her sneaking peeks at ill papi again. Ky was right—that showed no self-respect on her part.

"But picture it completely empty. All bare. It would be like walking into a scene from a horror movie," Ky explained. "You'd know that someone was going to jump out at you with a knife for sure."

"I'd be willing to risk it for a house like this," Sammi said.

"You one of those girls who wants a mansion?" Ky asked.

"One of *those* girls?" Sammi repeated. "Don't you think most people would like a mansion? Especially one right on the beach?"

"I can think of something I want more," Ky answered. His eyes flickered to her lips for one quick second.

"Oh, really?" Sammi asked. Her heart started beating a little faster.

"Yeah, really." Ky pulled her closer.

"Liiike, a plasma TV?" she asked teasingly, because she absolutely knew that wasn't what he was talking about.

"Huh-uh." Ky maneuvered her away from the crowd toward a darkened corner of the room.

"Liiike, an Escalade?" she teased.

"Huh-uh." They were barely moving now. Just swaying together.

"Liiike, a—"

"Like this," Ky told her. He lowered his head, hesitated for a moment, then his lips were on hers.

But even while Ky was kissing her—and she was liking it—there was one thing she couldn't help but wonder . . .

How would it feel to kiss ill papi?

"Come on," ill papi said. "I want to get something to drink." He tugged Sophie out of the huge room where the DJ was set up.

"He's playing my favorite song," Sophie protested.

"He'll play it again," ill papi said. "Every DJ plays that song at least five times a night." He led the way down the hall, then stopped in front of a closed door. "What do you think's in here?"

"Um, the poodle's bedroom?" Sophie suggested.

"Let's check it out." Ill papi pushed open the door.

"Guess it's not the poodle's. Unless the poodle is also into sewing," Sophie said. The room was dominated by a sewing machine and shelves loaded with bolts of fabric, plus all kinds of yarn and embroidery thread.

Ill papi sat down in one of the brocade chairs over by the windows and stretched his legs out in front of him. Huh? What was he doing? Sophie had no clue, but she went over and sat in the chair next to his. He seemed so serious all of a sudden. "So, what's up?" she asked. "Are you thinking of taking up knitting? It's supposed to be very trendy. All the celebs do it. The girl celebs. Haven't heard of many of the guys doing it, though. Which would make you quite the trendsetter."

"That day that we went to meet my . . . J-Bang?" ill papi began.

"Yeah, that day," Sophie said. "I had pancakes. The

waitress was cranky." She thought that trying to keep things light might help ill papi say . . . whatever he needed to say.

"When I got home, my mom wanted to know where I'd been, and I made up some story," ill papi confessed. "I knew if I told her I saw J-Bang, she'd have to, like, go to bed for a week and cry. Or buy a bunch of new clothes and go out every night looking for a new boyfriend. She definitely would have freaked in some way."

"I get why you didn't tell her." And Sophie totally did. That was a situation where a little lie wasn't such a bad thing.

"I guess. Except, she does that stuff half the time, anyway. She's either crying 'cause she has no guy, or crying 'cause she doesn't like the way the guy she has treats her. Or she's all crazy trying to find a guy." Ill papi shook his head. "That's why I shut down Sammi when she asked me out that time."

"What?" Sophie exclaimed, sounding way more horrified than she meant to. Ill papi didn't seem to notice.

"Like I told you—I didn't want to get all sucked into that junk. The way my mom is. But I just saw Ky and Sammi kissing in there . . ." He let his words trail off.

"Ky and Sammi were kissing?" Sophie hadn't noticed. She didn't usually notice all that much when she was with ill papi. Except ill papi.

"Yeah. And it felt like somebody punched me in the gut

when I saw them," ill papi went on.

Kind of how I feel right now, Sophie thought.

"I didn't want to like anyone. I don't. Except, seeing that—seeing her with another guy . . ." Ill papi couldn't finish again.

"So, what are you going to do? Maybe you should tell her—" Sophie began, trying really hard to be ill papi's friend.

"No. No, I was right when I turned her down. I wanted to go out with her. I totally wanted to. But I was right not to. I can't get sucked in," ill papi answered. "So I'm just not going to."

Ill papi liked Sammi. He *liked* liked her so much. It was as clear as those huge letters on the Hollywood sign.

And something else was clear to Sophie, too. There was no way ill papi was ever going to be able to stop liking her sister, no matter what he said.

Sammi couldn't get comfortable. She'd been lying in bed next to Sophie for what felt like twelve hours and she wasn't even close to falling asleep. The muscles in her back were tight, there was a lump in her pillow that was making her neck hurt, and a spot between her big toe and the one next to it wouldn't stop itching.

"You still awake, Soph?" she asked softly.

"Kinda," Sophie answered.

"Are Em and Chloe asleep?" Sammi thought it might help to talk things over with her sis. But she didn't want their conversation to turn into a group discussion.

"Yeah, I think so," Sophie said.

"Can I talk to you for a minute?" Sammi asked, stalling. She wanted to word-vomit at Sophie. But her feelings were all so jumbled up. And she was kind of ashamed of some of them.

"Mmm-hmm." Sophie rolled over to face her. "What?"

"You know Ky?" She knew she was still stalling. But she couldn't help it.

"Ky? As in Ky Miggs? From Hip Hop Kidz? Now sleeping in a room down the hall?" Sophie replied.

"Yeah. Well, he kissed me tonight," Sammi admitted.

"And?" Sophie prompted after a long moment of silence.

"And . . . and it was nice," Sammi said.

"Just nice? Huh."

"Nice plus. Or whatever word is one above nice," Sammi corrected. "But here's the deal. And it's stupid. I know that already. So you don't have to tell me. The deal is, I kept wondering how it would be to kiss ill papi."

Sophie didn't comment, and Sammi rushed on. "I know, I know, I know that it is so stupid. Because you already told me that ills doesn't want to like a girl like that. In a more-than-friends way. And he turned me down that time I asked him to the movies. So I should just be happy to be Ky's sort-of girlfriend—or getting to be Ky's girlfriend maybe—right? Since Ky is so fun to hang with. And cute. And pretty much all the good things you could want in a boy. So I should just be happy to keep things going with him, right? Right, Sophie?"

Sophie's only answer was a long, whistling snore.

Thanks a lot, Soph, Sammi thought. *Way to be there for your sister.*

Should I give another snore? Sophie asked herself. *No, that would be overkill.* She concentrated on taking deep, even, sleeping-person breaths, all while feeling like one of the most rotten people on earth. Or at least in L.A. Her sister wanted to talk to her about important stuff, and Sophie was pretending to snore.

It was all that she could think to do when Sammi started talking about ill papi, and how she wondered what he kissed like, and all that.

A good sister would have told Sammi every single thing that ill papi had said tonight. About how he really liked her.

But Sophie couldn't. She just couldn't. And she didn't want to lie. So she snored.

CHAPTER 8

Gloria and Devane faced off halfway up the stone steps leading to the rehearsal space all the hip-hop crews were using to get ready for the nationals. Devane scowled at her friend, then hauled back her fist and punched Gloria in the jaw.

"Did you get that?" Devane called down to Sophie, who was holding Devane's disposable camera.

"Got it," Sophie called back. She started up the stairs.

"Wait. One more," Gloria told her. "Now it's my turn to hit Devane." She grinned. "I can't believe these are the steps where they filmed the fight scene at the end of *Danger Is My Middle Name.*" She slugged Devane lightly in the stomach and Devane made an exaggerated *ooof* face for the camera. "I love that movie," Gloria added.

"It's so cool how everywhere you go in L.A., there's someplace you've seen on TV or in a movie or on a billboard," Devane said. "I really believed this building was a courthouse in New York when I saw *Danger.* And there are actually palm trees ten feet away that you just never saw onscreen." She shook her head.

Sophie trotted up the steps and handed off the camera. "I'm going inside to hit the soda machine. You two coming?"

"We'll catch you in there," Gloria said. "There's something I want to show Dee-Vee." She plopped down on one of the steps, and Devane sat next to her. She watched as Gloria started rooting through her huge canvas tote bag.

"Are you planning to spend the night here?" Devane asked. "You have enough stuff to."

"And I need it all," Gloria answered as she piled a paperback book, three lipsticks, a half-eaten candy bar, a tube of sunscreen, a coffee mug, a bottle of water, a mirror in a clear plastic case, and a stuffed cat between her and Devane. "Here it is," she announced. She pulled out a worn flowered scrapbook held together with a purple rubber band.

"What is that?" Devane asked.

Gloria flipped through the pages until she found the one she was looking for. "Here it is. A letter from you. 'Dear Emily Rose,' " Gloria began to read. "'You're not going to believe this—'"

"You saved that?" Devane exclaimed. "I saved mine, too—a bunch of the ones you wrote—for a long time. Then Tamal—never mind. I dealt with him. I can't believe you have that letter."

"I can't believe we were dorky enough to write letters back and forth from our make-believe younger sisters," Gloria replied.

"It was your dorky idea."

"Nuh-uh. You were the dorky one."

"No, you were," Devane insisted.

"It was kind of fun, wasn't it?" Gloria asked.

Devane smiled. "Yeah. That's why my idea was so great."

Gloria laughed, then started shoving all her junk back in her purse. "I've got to get in there. The Shoowops are scheduled for practice in about five minutes." She tore out one page of the letter and handed it to Devane. "Tell Tamal if anything happens to this, he'll have to deal with me. And I'm much scarier than you."

"You're so not," Devane said as they headed inside.

"I so am," Gloria shot back. "I'm extremely scary. You cross me, and watch out."

"My practice starts in four minutes, and there's something I've been wanting to ask you for almost an hour," Flash admitted to Emerson. They were sitting in the hallway across from the room where the Shoowops—then later the Hip Hop Kidz—would be rehearsing.

"Uh-oh," Emerson said. "Should I be scared?"

"No," Flash answered quickly. "At least, I don't think so."

He didn't say anything else.

"I think you're down to three minutes," Emerson told him.

"Give me a break. I never asked anyone out before," Flash said. He grinned at her. "So will you go out with me? It's all very parent-approved. My parents have tickets to a show at the Disney concert hall tonight that they can't use. They said it was okay if I asked you. They'll arrange a car service for us and everything."

Emerson felt herself start to grin, too. "That would be great." The grin almost immediately began to slide off her face. "But I don't think my parents—"

"Wait. You want to go, right?" Flash asked.

"Yes. I absolutely want to go," Emerson said. How could she not want to go?

"Okay." He stared up at the ceiling for a moment, thinking. Emerson had no idea what he was thinking about. "Okay, you said your mom was on some kind of arts council, right?"

Emerson nodded, baffled.

"Did she ever do a silent auction for it?" Flash asked.

"Yeah, last year," Emerson answered.

Flash pulled out his cell phone and pressed a speed dial number. "Mom, hey," he said into the phone. "I just found somebody for you to talk to about the silent auction you're going to arrange for the junior league. Emerson's mom ran a silent auction last year. You should call her up."

Emerson heard his mother answering, but she couldn't make out the words. "What's your home phone?" Flash asked Em.

She gave it to him, and he passed it on to his mom. "When you call, would you ask Mrs. Lane's permission for Emerson to go with me to the concert tonight? Convince her that I'm trustworthy and everything." Emerson heard Flash's mother's voice again, then Flash said, "Thanks, Mom," and hung up.

"All set," he told her. "My mother would have called even without the auction as an extra reason, but this way the two of them will bond. I'm sure your mom will say yes."

Emerson believed him. And that meant tonight, she was going to have her first date. The dance with Wes didn't count. It might have been her first official date. But the concert with Flash would be her first *real* date.

"Wow. Look at Flash go," Sophie said to Sammi. They both stood watching the Shoowops begin their rehearsal.

"He's not as good as ill papi," Sammi answered. Then she gave a groan of frustration. "Why does that keep happening? Why does everything make me think of him? I hate that!"

Sammi sounded so upset. She really liked ill papi. The

way he really liked her.

Sophie opened her mouth to tell her sister the truth. But what came out was, "Maybe you're trying too hard *not* to think of him. Sometimes when I tell myself not to think about something, it ends up being *all* I can think about."

"Yeah, maybe," Sammi agreed. She wrapped one arm around Sophie's shoulders. "Thanks, Soph."

She's thanking me for lying to her, Sophie thought miserably. No, not for lying, really. But almost. Not telling something so big was pretty much lying.

Except it wasn't as if ill papi had changed his mind about *liking* someone. He still didn't want to go into the *like* zone at all, ever. So it wasn't like Sophie was really keeping Sammi and ill papi apart by not saying anything.

"Did you see that flip the guy with the fauxhawk just did?" M.J. exclaimed as he joined them at the window.

"Yeah," Devane answered as she took a spot at the window. "His name is Slider. I met him last night when I was hanging with Gloria." She shook her head. "He wasn't pulling out any moves like that when I saw him. He'd found one of the Harper's computers and was all into his fantasy football team. Who knew he could bring it?"

"He's not the only one," Fridge said as he stepped up behind Sophie. "See that girl in the shirt with a crown on it? She can do a headspin that won't quit. I saw her last night on the dance floor upstairs."

The Shoowops launched into the routine Sophie and the others had seen on tape. They were so high-octane, it was like they were about to set the floor on fire.

"They're good," M.J. said.

"Scary good," Sophie agreed.

Devane hated that Gloria was watching the Hip Hop Kidz rehearse. Most of the Shoowops were crowded around the window, too, and Devane wasn't happy they were seeing this mess the Kidz were serving up as dancing today. But she really hated that Gloria was getting any eyeful of her crew at their worst.

You shouldn't even be thinking about her, Devane told herself as she launched into the final sequence for the fourth time. *Focus on your moves.*

And she did. Or she tried to. But she still felt *off*. It didn't help when Fridge launched into his final position half a beat early and ended up whacking her in the ribs.

"All right, that was—" Gina pulled in a long breath.

"That was awful," Rachel said for her.

"It definitely wasn't your best," Gina agreed. "But you've got to expect to be nervous. We're at the nationals. It's the big time. Just think of today as getting all that nervousness out of your system. I guarantee that when you get on the stage tomorrow, it will all come together. That's what all our rehearsing and work has been for."

The Shoowops haven't been showing any nerves, Devane thought. *And this is the big time for them, too.*

"Don't sweat it, you guys," M.J. called out. "It's just because I'm not wearing the socks. I didn't want to use up the luck on a rehearsal. They'll be fully charged tomorrow, and we're going to dominate!"

That got some "yeahs" and some applause. But Devane didn't think the crew was completely convinced of their power to dominate. Not after watching the other team rehearse.

"Now, I'm going to have you guys each do your solos. I want to see them one more time before I slot them in for tomorrow's performance," Gina told them.

You're getting a solo, Devane told herself. *Whatever it is that's off, you get it back on. Now.*

She watched as M.J. did his solo. All power moves. Not that original. But it was still the kind of thing that would drive a crowd mad. He'd really gotten his jackhammer down. And without ills in the competition, the Hip Hop Kidz needed someone who could bring the old-school moves. And that was M.J.

There were four solos in their routine. M.J. would probably get one of them. Very probably. And Devane suspected Emerson's hip-hop ballet stylings would get one of the others.

Gina motioned Max to the middle of the floor. Max

went for an almost all-krumping solo. The perfect choice for someone who couldn't stand still, even when she wanted to. Good. But not special. *I'm better than she is*, Devane thought. *There's no way Max gets a solo over me.*

"You're up, Devane," Gina called. *Time to let it out*, Devane told herself. *Don't hold anything back. Not one ounce of energy.*

Devane served up a variation of the blocking and hinging she'd started playing with that day at the block party, focusing with every nerve and cell in her body.

She held the final pose and the room came into focus around her. Gloria looked impressed out there on the other side of the window. Devane grinned at her as she stepped out of her freeze. *I've learned a few things since the fourth grade, Glow*, Devane thought. *You better watch yourself!*

Except it was clear that Gloria had learned a few things, too. And her whole crew was sizzlin'. Devane couldn't say that about her group. Not at this rehearsal, anyway.

Chloe took the floor, and Devane turned her attention over to Chloe's moves. She decided that Chloe's solo was a little better than Max's. And that maybe she was even as good as M.J. But Devane was still sure M.J. was going to get one of the slots. And she was sure she was, too.

"Okay, here's how it's gonna go down," Gina called after all the dancers had taken their best shot. "First solo, Fridge." Devane could get that. There was something about Fridge.

He didn't have the best technique of anyone in the group, but when he moved, you wanted to watch.

"Second, Emerson." Devane nodded. She'd been expecting the ballerina to get picked. And . . . yeah, she deserved it.

"Third . . ." Gina paused to check her notes. Devane felt the muscles in her shoulders tighten. She concentrated on keeping an I'm-so-not-worried expression on her face. "Third, Devane," Gina continued. "And for the fourth solo, M.J. That's it, guys. That was our last rehearsal before we compete. Remember to sign up with Randall if you want to hit Grauman's Chinese Theatre tonight. Or me if you want to do the Grove. And yes, you have to do one or the other."

Emerson raised her hand. "Right—your mom called twenty minutes ago. I have you down as going to the Disney concert hall with Charles Harper," Gina told her. "We'll be back before you are, so just come straight to Maddy's and my room and check in, okay?"

Em nodded. *Hmm. How'd she score that?* Devane wondered. *Mommy and Daddy pull some strings?* Not that Devane wouldn't rather go to Grauman's. Her photo collection wouldn't be complete without a shot of her pressing her hands into the cement in front of that theater, like a million stars had done.

"The van will be out front in half an hour to take you back to the motel," Gina finished up. "Go on and get changed.

Good work, everybody!"

Yeah, right, Devane thought. Nobody else seemed to believe Gina, either. Every person Devane looked at seemed to be deep in thought. And not happy thoughts. More like, I-can't-believe-I-just-messed-up-like-that thoughts.

Devane opened the door to the practice room. The Shoowops who had been watching had disappeared. Devane was glad she didn't have to come up with something to say to Gloria right now.

"I didn't really think anyone could beat us. I didn't walk around saying it, but that's actually what I thought," Chloe admitted as they headed toward the locker room. "But, you guys, I think the Shoowops could beat us."

The words sent a bolt of ice through Devane's body. Because she thought they might be true.

CHAPTER 9

"We can still go on to world even if we don't beat them," Sophie reminded everyone as she untied her sneakers in the locker room. "Three teams from the varsity category get to move on."

"You're saying you don't want to win world?" Devane asked. "That it would be okay with you to squeak through the nationals and *then* get taken down by the Shoowops? We'd be going home losers."

"Not exactly losers," Sophie muttered. "And that's not what I'm saying. I'm saying that we don't just have one chance to beat the Shoowops. I'm saying the Shoowops are fierce, but so are we." She curled her hands into claws. "We're supah fierce. And if we don't beat them on Friday, then we *will* beat them at world."

"If we make it to the top three," Becca said quietly.

"I'm thinking it wouldn't hurt if the Shoowops were to somehow just disappear from the competition," Rachel joked. "In an Act of God kind of way."

"You mean like a bolt of lightning?" Emerson asked.

"Well, maybe something a little less Act of God, and a little more Act of Hip Hop Kidz," Rachel admitted.

Chloe gave a mad-scientist cackle. "I'm liking this. We could, uh, hide all their shoes."

"And all the shoes in L.A.? That's a lot of shoes," Sophie teased. "But we could, hmm, we could put poison ivy in all their shoes. It's hard to dance great if you're all itchy."

"Unless their itching makes them twitch in some cool way." Max did some itchy-twitchy moves to illustrate.

"Yeah, if we're going to do this, we have to do it right. I'm thinking—" Devane noticed Max repeatedly jerking her head toward the door, eyes wide. Devane looked over—and saw Gloria, eyes narrowed.

"Go on, Dee-Vee," Gloria said. "I'd like to hear this."

"We were just playing, Glow," Devane told her friend. "And you could have coughed or something to let us know you were there, instead of eavesdropping."

"I wasn't eavesdropping," Gloria insisted. "I came in here to go to the bathroom. Or isn't that allowed?"

Devane rolled her eyes. Gloria was still a little bit of a drama girl. That hadn't changed. "Of course it's allowed. Now are you going to blow this thing up until it's ready for E!, or are you going to—"

"What I'm going to do is my business," Gloria said as she walked past the Hip Hop Kidz girls. When she reached the bathroom door, she looked over her shoulder at Devane. "I thought you were my friend."

Max gave up the expected "Oooh." Somebody had to.

Devane stood up. Miss Gloria could not actually believe she could say that to Devane and just walk away. "I'll be right back," she told the other girls.

"Oooh!" Max called out again. This time Chloe joined in. *Oooh is right*, Devane thought as she strode over to the bathroom. She threw open the door just as Gloria was about to step into one of the stalls.

"Don't even think about hiding in there," Devane ordered. "Because we both know I *will* come in and get you."

Gloria placed her hands on her hips. "I'm quaking."

Devane couldn't stop herself from smiling. Gloria used to use that "I'm quaking" expression all the time back in Florida. "Glow, come on, we were just trash-talking. You guys are the competition. You know how it goes."

"It didn't sound like trash talk. It sounded like you were making plans," Gloria insisted.

"Come on. Stealing everybody's shoes? That's a plan?" Devane shot back.

"You were about to come up with something else. Something real." Gloria's eyes were chilly as she looked at Devane.

"You've seen me dance," Devane answered. "I don't need any help winning. I can bring it all on my own, and you know that."

"What I know is that you've always cared more about winning than anything else," Gloria answered. "How do I know that doesn't mean cheating?"

"I can't believe you actually think I would cheat." Devane stared at her for a long moment, then shook her head in disgust. "You know what, Gloria, I thought you were my friend."

There was a hush as the Los Angeles Philharmonic played the last notes of Beethoven's Symphony No. 8. Then everyone in the theater broke into loud applause.

"Do you want to go get something to drink?" Flash asked when the clapping had tapered off and the crowd dispersed for intermission.

"Sure," Emerson said.

They walked up the aisle, the ceiling above them almost seeming to billow like a tapestry. The outside of the concert hall had the feeling of motion, too. It reminded Emerson of sails, all sizes of sails, blowing in the wind, sails made out of sheets of metal. "I'm glad you were able to come with me tonight," Flash said after they'd gotten their sodas and stepped out into the night air.

"Thanks for asking me," Emerson answered. *We both sound so perfect,* she thought. *He could be Wes. And I could* be . . . *the Emerson my mom wishes I was, the one who always does absolutely everything correctly in the way that makes the most people happy.*

She glanced over at Flash. He didn't look exactly happy. He looked like he wished he could get out of there. Out of there and away from her.

"If I see your mom, I'll make sure to tell her you were the perfect host," Emerson said, trying to remind him of their conversation yesterday, when they were having a good time. A really great time. At least that's what Emerson had thought.

"Cool, yeah, that would be good," Flash muttered. Em wasn't sure he'd even heard exactly what she'd said.

"Is something wrong?" she blurted out. "You're acting kind of weird."

"I know. Sorry. I guess I should just ask you." Flash took a long swallow of his soda.

"Ask me what?" Emerson shook her head. She didn't think it was going to be anything good this time. Not like this afternoon when he'd asked her out. That somehow felt like a million years ago. "Doesn't matter. Just ask."

"So does your crew have something planned to try to keep the Shoowops out of the nationals?" Flash asked, his face solemn.

"No. No way," Emerson assured him. "Gloria told you that, right?"

Flash nodded.

"Here's the deal. She overheard some of the girls in the locker room goofing about ways to keep you guys out of the competitions—'cause we all think the Shoowops are smoking. But we weren't serious," Emerson explained. "My best friend, Sophie, was one of the girls doing the talking, and Sophie is always joking around. Only about every third word out of her mouth is meant to be for real."

"We have a Sophie on our crew. Except he's a guy—Vince," Flash admitted.

"And Devane was one of the other girls," Emerson went on. "There's no way Devane would ever sabotage another crew. Devane thinks she's a better dancer than anyone who's ever been born or will be born. She might not think the rest of the Hip Hop Kidz group is as good as the Shoowops. But I'm sure she thinks she can carry us through the competition on her talent alone."

Flash laughed. "We have a Devane type, too. Her name is Princess—just Princess."

"Devane doesn't go for the last name thing, either. When you're very special, one name is all you need," Emerson told Flash. "So, do you have an Emerson Lane on your crew?"

Flash tilted his head to one side, pretending to consider. "You're pretty unique, I think." He touched her arm quickly. "Sorry I even thought your group might trash the Shoowops. That wasn't cool of me."

"It's okay. It's not like you really know us," Emerson answered.

"I want to, though. You think maybe we can get together tomorrow night? You're going to be watching the other crews perform during the day, aren't you?" Flash asked.

"Yeah. I mean, yes, I'm going to be watching the other crews, since we don't perform until Friday. And, yes, it would be fun to do something with you. I just have to check with Gina. But she'll probably say yes again if my mom calls like she did about the concert. I know my mom will say yes. She called me as soon as she got off the phone with your mom and was raving about her."

"Excellent." The lights in the lobby dimmed and a soft chime sounded. "We've got to go back in."

Is this what it's like to have a boyfriend? Emerson wondered as they headed back to their seats. She'd never had a boyfriend before, and she'd practically just met Flash.

Though, somehow, he still kind of felt boyfriend-like. And she liked it.

CHAPTER 10

"You guys go on without me," Sophie told Emerson, Chloe, and Sammi as they headed into the Redondo Beach Performing Arts Center to watch the first day of the nationals. "I see someone I know."

Someone she sort of knew, at least. Ill papi's dad was gesturing to her from across the lobby full of hip-hoppers and hip-hop fans. Sophie hurried over to him. "Hey," she said.

"Hi." He ran his hands over his shaved head. "Hi," he repeated. "Look, I wanted you to know that I hated how things went down when I met you and Tim—ill papi—for brunch."

"O-kay," Sophie said slowly. "But why are you telling me? Not that I mind or anything. But isn't this something you should be telling ill papi?"

"I tried. Or I was going to try. I didn't even get that far. He walked right by me a couple minutes ago. I was out here waiting for him. I know he saw me, but he wouldn't stop.

Like he didn't even know me."

He doesn't *even know you.* Sophie kept the thought to herself. It was too mean to say out loud, even though J-Bang had done so many very uncool things.

"I didn't want to make a scene about it, especially in front of his friends," J-Bang continued, then he hesitated, looking down at his feet like a little boy. "That's why I'm talking to you." He raised his eyes to meet Sophie's. "Can you help me out? Convince ill papi to give me another chance? I know I don't deserve it. But I want to try and get something started with him. Get to know him. He's . . . he is my kid."

"I'll talk to him," Sophie answered. "But I'm not going to try and make ill papi do anything he doesn't want to do."

"I get that. I'm not asking you to," J-Bang answered quickly.

"You really hurt him, you know that, right?" Sophie asked.

"Yeah. Yeah. I think I'm finally starting to understand that. I thought that since he probably didn't remember me, what did it matter . . ." J-Bang cleared his throat. "I need to get inside. We're going to be starting up in about fifteen minutes." He met her gaze. "Whatever ill papi decides, I'll go with it. Just try to get him to talk to me, Sophie. Just one more time."

Devane tried to ignore the fact that Gloria and all her Shoowop crew were sitting one row in front of her and the other Hip Hop Kidz. Today wasn't about them. Today was about watching the other groups competing in the nationals—and trying to move on to world.

A crew called The Team took the stage. They were dressed in a mix of hip-hop gear and baseball uniforms, and they used baseball bats throughout the routine, tossing the bats back and forth, jumping over them, beating out rhythms with them. *It must have taken a lot of practice for the dancers to move between flying hunks of wood so easily*, Devane thought, trying to watch them like a judge would.

An all-girl crew from Texas was up next. While the Shoowops had worked in some swing, this group had added a little Western flava by mixing it up with some line dancing. And a locking version of what Devane was pretty sure was bull-riding.

"They are smokin'," M.J. said from a couple seats down as the crowd gave it up for the Cowbelles. "Just watching them makes me have to touch my lucky socks." He unzipped his backpack.

J-Bang jogged out onstage with his mike. "Can I get a yee-haw for my girls?" A bunch of dorks in the crowd gave him one. "Next up, we've got the Graffiti Artists, from New Jersey."

They were just way too plastic, Devane decided. She

doubted anyone on that crew had ever danced anywhere but in a studio. Or tried anything that hadn't been choreographed for them. There was no way the Graffiti Artists were moving on to world, no possible way.

"My socks aren't in here," Devane heard M.J. mutter. A couple seconds later, he upended his backpack in Fridge's lap.

"Hey!" Fridge protested.

"I need to look for them," M.J. explained, not bothering to keep his voice down even though the Grafitti Artists were still serving up their stale moves.

"Not on me you don't, bro," Fridge insisted.

"It'll only take a second." M.J., who was usually cooler than cool, sounded like he was about to lose it. "They aren't here!" he exclaimed. "They really aren't here!"

And now he had totally lost it.

Gloria turned around. *Shhh. It's the middle of a performance.*

"She did this." M.J. leaned toward Gloria. "What did you do with my lucky socks?"

Emerson exchanged a what-are-we-supposed-to-do? look with Flash, who was sitting right in front of her.

You're the one in M.J.'s group. You're the one who has to deal, she told herself. "M.J.—" That was all she got out.

Because an usher who looked intimidating enough to be a bouncer was pointing at the entire row of Hip Hop Kidz, then pointing toward the door.

"You're kicking the wrong people out," M.J. protested as the crowd broke into applause for the Graffiti Artists. "That girl stole something from me, something very valuable."

"A stinky pair of socks," Gloria shot back. "Which I did not steal."

"She stole them because she knows we're going to kick booty when we compete tomorrow, and she'll do anything to try to take us down," Max cut in, leaping to her feet.

"Like we're going to need any help to flatten you," the guy next to Gloria told Max.

"All right," the bouncer-shaped usher snapped. "All of you. Both teams. Out. Or I'll make sure none of you will perform tomorrow."

"That's no—" Chloe began.

"Let's just do it," Emerson begged. "We came all this way. We don't want to lose before we even start." She gave Soph a gentle push, and Sophie started toward the aisle. That got everybody—from both crews—moving out of the auditorium as J-Bang started introducing the next act.

"I can't believe we got kicked out. I'm going home," the Shoowop with the fauxhawk—Slider—said as soon as the heavy auditorium doors swung shut behind them.

"No one is going anywhere until I find out what happened

to my socks," M.J. announced.

"Yeah, just give them back. And while you're at it, do you think you guys could grow a sense of humor?" Rachel asked. "We were just goofing in the locker room. We weren't going to actually do anything to you."

"I told you that," Devane jumped in, getting in Gloria's face. "But you obviously decided you couldn't trust me. You had to get your new friends to strike first, before we could do what we had planned to you—which was nothing. Noth-ing."

"We've seen you dance," the boy who'd been sitting next to Gloria said. "And we all know we don't need anything to help us burn you to ash."

"Zach's right," Gloria said. "And anyway, how would any of us even know that Ace over there had lucky socks?"

"Exactly," added a girl in a T-shirt with a crown on it—a different color than the one she'd had on at rehearsal yesterday. She had to be Princess, Emerson decided.

There was a long moment of silence. Emerson thought the whole thing was going to end right then and there.

But Devane slowly turned her head toward Em. Then so did M.J. And Max. And Fridge. And Rachel.

"What?" Emerson cried.

"Well, you're a good choice for the leak," Devane told her. "Flash is your boyfriend."

"He's not . . ." Emerson hesitated. She didn't know what

they were. "We're friends."

"Friends who go off to fancy concerts without inviting the rest of us," Devane interrupted.

"There were only two tickets," Flash protested. "My parents couldn't use them."

"So nice to have a rich mommy and daddy," Devane said. "Ballerina here has them, too. Are you sure you didn't *accidentally* let something slip, like on the limo ride home?"

CHAPTER 11

Emerson leaned against the side of the auditorium and sucked in a long, shaky breath, trying to calm down. She looked around. The sky was sky blue, the sun a picture-book yellow ball set off by a few cottony white clouds. It was a perfect day. But Emerson felt like her whole world was cracking apart.

"She didn't mean it, Em," Sophie said as she slipped outside and joined Emerson.

"Yeah, she did." Emerson leaned her head back against the warm wall and sighed. "She did. She actually thinks I'd do something to hurt the group."

Emerson shoved herself away from the building. "It was just like before. From the beginning, Devane looked at me and saw some rich blond girl who came from a whole different universe. Somebody she couldn't trust. Forget about be friends with."

"But she *is* your friend now," Sophie protested.

"Is she out here talking to me?" Emerson asked. "No,

you are. That shows who's my friend." She shook her head. "What makes me extra crazy is that Devane knows what I went through to get here with my parents and everything. She's the one who convinced them to let me back in the group until the nationals and world are over. How can she believe even for a second I'd do anything to mess up something so important? These competitions are the last times I'm ever going to be dancing with the Hip Hop Kidz."

"She has some kind of brain impairment," Sophie said. "She talks first, thinks later. If she thought first, she'd know that you wouldn't have given any info to Flash that might hurt the crew. Nobody else in the group thinks you would."

Emerson raised her eyebrows. "Are you sure? I was getting some intense evil looks from quite a few people."

"Well, anybody who was looking at you like that is a poo-head. And I'm not afraid to tell them so," Sophie insisted. She turned toward the door. "Uh-oh. We've got company."

"Devane?" Emerson asked. But when she looked around, she saw Flash waving at her.

"You know I completely trust you—like with my unborn children, and my secret stash of mini peanut butter cups, right?" Sophie asked.

"Yeah. Of course," Emerson told her.

"Good. So don't take this the wrong way," Sophie went on. "I wouldn't let anybody in either crew see you and Flash together right now. Just pretend you're Romeo and Juliet.

But skip the part where they both die."

Sophie marched back inside and around to the main lobby. The Shoowops and the Hip Hop Kidz were still going at it. "Enough!" Sophie barked when she reached them. "We're never going to agree on what exactly happened to M.J.'s socks." She looked at him. "Like it even matters. The only thing those socks do is make your whole body smell like toe jam. And that's not lucky for anybody."

"We completely blew it at rehearsal yesterday when M.J. wasn't wearing the socks," Max exclaimed.

"Oh, is *that* why you sucked?" Slider asked.

"And he was wearing them when we won the regionals," Fridge added, ignoring the guy. "Right, M.J.?"

"And the day I got into—"

"Yeah, yeah," Sophie cut in. "I say socks have nothing to do with whether we win or lose. But whatever. Ill papi, can I talk to you away from the possible blood-splatter zone?"

Ill papi followed Sophie up the stairs. They sat down on one of the padded benches in the second-floor lobby. "I saw J-Bang this morning," she said, wanting to just get it out there.

"So did I," ills answered. "He acted like he expected me to come over and say hi or something."

"Yeah. Well. I did talk to him for a minute." Sophie tensed

up, hoping ill papi wouldn't stand up and walk away from her the way he'd walked away from J-Bang at the restaurant.

"Why?" Ill papi didn't sound happy, but his behind was still on the bench, so that was something.

"I don't know. Maybe I shouldn't have. Here's the thing, though—he wanted me to ask you to give him another chance." Sophie looked over at ill papi, trying to read the expression on his face. It was like someone had flipped his off switch. He just seemed . . . empty.

"Another chance for what?" ills muttered. His voice sounded empty, too. "It's too late for him to be my dad."

"I think just to get to know you. For you to get to know him. I guess for now, he wants another chance to talk to you," Sophie said. "I told him I'd pass the message on, but that I wouldn't try to convince you to do anything you didn't want to do."

"What if I don't know what I want to do?" ill papi asked.

"Don't you?"

"Right now I never want to see him again. He basically said he didn't think about me for eleven years. Who knows if he ever would have thought of me if I hadn't called him?" Ill papi snorted. "I don't know what I was expecting. What reason did I think he'd have for taking off? He was wanted by the mob and didn't want to put me in danger? He had some kind of disease he didn't want me to catch?" He shook his head. "I actually used to think things like that.

What a fool I am."

"I used to think I was adopted and that I was actually heir to the Reese's Peanut Butter Cup fortune—which I thought was all Reese's Peanut Butter Cups," Sophie said, trying to make him laugh. Although it was true. She had thought that for a while.

"That's not really the same," ill papi said.

"It sort of is. Anyway, you said you didn't know what you wanted to do. But it sounds like you do. It sounds like you don't want to see him," Sophie said.

"Not now," ill papi agreed. "But someday, maybe. Like when I'm living on my own . . ."

"You should write him a letter." Sophie unzipped her backpack and started rooting around for paper. "That way you won't have to actually talk to him. But you can still say what you want to say . . . about maybe someday wanting to get in touch."

"I'm not that great at writing," ill papi told her.

"Okay, you talk. I'll write," Sophie offered. She found a few sheets of unwrinkled paper and a pen, then waited.

"I don't want to talk to you now," ill papi dictated. Sophie thought maybe he should start with "Dear J-Bang" or even "Dear Dad," but she didn't say anything. She didn't want to interrupt ill papi's flow.

"I don't want to see you. I don't know if I ever will. You left me, and you didn't even try to see me. I thought maybe you'd have an explanation. But you don't. Maybe someday I'll be up for talking to you. I'll find you if I do. You don't get to try to find me." Ill papi stared down at the floor, like there might be some more—or some better—words written there. He shrugged. "I guess I'll just sign my name. I can't think of anything else."

Sophie handed the paper and pen over. Ill papi signed without reading the letter and thrust it back at her. "It's not like he should care. He went this long without talking to me."

"So you want me to give it to him?" she asked.

"Yeah. I guess. Yeah," ill papi said.

Sophie carefully folded the letter and slid it into the outside pocket of her backpack. "Should we go back downstairs? See if there's any blood that needs to be cleaned up, or if we need to call an ambulance or anything?"

"Do you care if we just stay up here for a while?" Ill papi still sounded all hollowed out.

"As long as you want," Sophie told him.

So they sat there, not talking. Because Sophie had the feeling talking was the last thing ill papi wanted to do. He was wrung out. He needed a chance to chill for a little bit, without having to even think.

When people started leaving the auditorium about twenty minutes later, Sophie decided it was time to speak. "Looks like they're on a break. Do you want me to try and find J-Bang now, or . . . ?"

"Yeah. I'll stay here."

Sophie stood up, grabbed her backpack, and headed downstairs. She noticed that both the Shoowops and the Hip Hop Kidz had disappeared from the lobby—or gotten kicked out of there, too. Whatever. Sophie couldn't deal with that right now. She walked into the auditorium, going against the current of people coming out.

J-Bang was easy to spot. He was up onstage talking to a couple of the judges. As soon as he saw Sophie coming down the aisle, he leaped off and rushed up to her. "Did you talk to him?" he asked.

"Uh-huh." Sophie hated to see the way J-Bang's eyes glittered with excitement—and hope. "He . . . he wrote you a note." She busied herself unzipping the front pocket of her backpack and pulling the letter out, so she could have a break from looking at J-Bang's face. As soon as she handed him the folded piece of paper, she started to turn to leave.

J-Bang caught her by the elbow. "Will you wait? In case there's an answer I want to send back?"

"Sure," Sophie said, trying to look like she had no idea what the letter said.

J-Bang let go of her arm and opened the letter. Sophie felt like she could see all that excitement and hope draining out of him with each word he read. Finally, he looked up at her. "Tell Tim—" He swallowed hard. "Tell him not to worry.

I won't ever try to talk to him again."

"We have to step up," Fridge told the group that was gathered by one of the palm trees in front of the auditorium. "No way can we let this happen without some retaliation. We all know they stole those socks."

"Then lied about it!" Max added.

"We have to do something," M.J. said. "We have to get the socks back. We're not going to win tomorrow without them. Forget about winning—we won't even be in the top three. There's no way we're moving on to world without the socks."

Devane felt like someone had taken a blowtorch to her body, like her blood had turned to scorching steam. Nobody messed with her crew and got away with it. Nobody. Especially Gloria Neely. And Gloria was the one who started all this. If the girl had any kind of sense of humor, she wouldn't have gone whining to the Shoowops. Gloria never had been able to tell when anybody was kidding.

Wait. That reminded Devane of something else she knew about Glow.

"I say we—" Adam began.

"—put Vaseline on the edges of the stage right before they go on," Allan concluded.

"Nah. I've got the perfect way for us to get revenge,

y'all," Devane told them. "I've known Gloria from way back. I just remembered something about Miss G that gives us the perfect way to send a message to the whole Shoowop crew."

CHAPTER 12

"Time for Operation Freak," Devane said, looking across the food court at the table the Shoowops had claimed. "Let's move it out." She stood up, locked her eyes on Gloria, and strode toward her. Max and M.J. followed.

"Oh, no. I am not seeing this." Zach stood up and glared at the three of them. "I am *not* seeing you Kidz coming right over to our table."

"We came for my socks," M.J. told him.

"You really must be insecure about your dancing if you're that worried about them," Princess observed, licking some frozen yogurt off her spoon.

"We told you we don't have them," Gloria protested, talking directly to Devane.

"Well, guess what, Glow Worm," Devane answered, using the nickname Gloria had hated when she was little. "We don't believe you."

Gloria's cheeks flushed. "You started this whole thing, Deranged," she shot back, using the nickname Devane had hated when *she* was little.

"I don't care who started it. I just want the socks," M.J. said. "Or I might have to do something about it."

Slider snorted. "Oh, right."

"Yeah!" Max exclaimed. "We might have to do something about it."

"Is she your bodyguard or what?" Zach asked M.J., jerking his head at Max, who weighed about ninety pounds.

All the Shoowops laughed. *Go for it*, Devane told herself. She took a super-fast look at the table behind her. Still empty. Then she planted her foot on Gloria's big canvas tote bag and slid it under the table. Chloe should be in position under there, ready to grab it and do what needed to be done.

"I don't need a bodyguard," M.J. told the Shoowops.

"Yeah, all he needs are his *luuucky* socks," Zach answered. "Tell us again. Did they have duckies on them? Or bunnies? Or duckies *and* bunnies?"

"*You* wear duckies and bunnies," Max yelled.

Devane tried not to roll her eyes. She'd chosen Max as the third person to come over to the table because Max was loud, and loud was good when you were trying to create a diversion. But "You wear duckies and bunnies"? That was just embarrassing for everybody.

"We're trying to eat here," Gloria told Devane. "You don't have anything new to say, so can you just go away?" She took a big bite of her salad.

Devane felt Gloria's tote hit her in the ankle. Chloe had done the dirty deed. This was Devane's cue. "Fine," she answered as she pushed the bag back next to Gloria's chair with her foot. She started away from the table, then turned back. "I shouldn't be telling you this, but since we used to be friends—you have a big piece of spinach stuck to one of your teeth. It looks foul."

And like clockwork, Gloria grabbed her tote and searched through it until she found her mirror in the plastic sleeve. The one Devane had seen when Gloria had showed her the scrapbook. The one Devane was counting on for this plan to work.

Devane tried not to smile as Gloria let out a long shriek. "What's wrong?" Devane asked.

"It's broken." The mirror fell from Gloria's trembling fingers. "It's broken." Her voice was trembling, too.

I knew she'd still have that thing about broken mirrors, Devane thought triumphantly. "Oooh. Your seven years of bad luck definitely won't be over before the nationals," she said.

"Somebody get this away from me." Gloria pushed the mirror into the middle of the table. "No!" she exclaimed when Zach reached for it.

"You just said—" Zach began.

"You have to use a napkin or something. Otherwise you'll get the bad luck all over you," Gloria told him. "If that happens, there's no way we can win tomorrow." She shook her head. "Even if you don't touch it, I probably have enough bad luck to make us come in last."

"Well, at least now we'll have a fair competition," Devane commented. "Both our crews have lost a little of their luck."

"You did this, Devane," Gloria accused.

"How could I have done it? You have your bag with you all the time, right?" Devane asked.

Gloria frowned. "Yeah," she muttered.

"So I guess you're just unlucky," Devane told her. She, M.J., and Max walked away before Gloria and the Shoowops came up with any answer.

"So, no hip-hop talk of any kind tonight, agreed? No Shoowop. No Kidz—" Flash began.

"No nationals, no world, no top rocks, no popping," Emerson added.

"Let's shake on it." He stuck out his hand and Emerson gave it three quick shakes. Then they walked onto the Santa Monica Pier.

"Want to try some fried avocado?" Flash asked. "Avocado is pretty much what makes any food Californian. California burger—that's a burger with avocado. California roll—sushi with avocado. So fried avocado—basically fried California."

"I kind of think I shouldn't be trying any weird fried food right before the—" Emerson caught herself before she said the word "competition." She didn't want to break their agreement already. "Before tomorrow. My stomach is especially sensitive on Fridays."

"Mine too," Flash agreed. "Pizza?"

"Yeah. Pizza is always good before Friday. And Monday. And Tuesday. Pizza is pretty much always good." Emerson followed Flash over to a little pizza stand on the boardwalk. A blast of yummy smell hit her in the face. "My parents would freak if they saw me eating here."

Flash laughed. "Mine too. I actually promised them I'd take you to that place over there." He pointed to a white-tablecloth kind of restaurant at the foot of the pier. "We can still go there if you want. Their treat."

"After I've smelled this pizza? No way." Emerson was sure Devane would've expected her to pick the white-tablecloth place. Devane thought she knew everything about Emerson, just because Emerson's parents had money. Emerson could still hardly believe Devane actually thought—

Flash waved his hand in front of her eyes. "Em? Did you hear the guy? What kind of pizza do you want?"

"Pepperoni," Emerson said. "Sorry."

"What were you thinking about?" Flash asked. "Your forehead got all crinkly."

Emerson couldn't come up with a good lie fast enough.

"The forbidden topic," she admitted.

"You need the Ferris wheel. No one can be at the top of that and think of anything but how cool it is up there." He took two slices of pizza on flimsy paper plates from the pizza guy and handed over some cash. "My parents gave me enough money for the restaurant we didn't go to, so I guess we'll have to spend it on the Ferris wheel and the ship that swings back and forth and ten-dollar games with two-dollar prizes and more food they wouldn't approve of."

Emerson laughed. "If we have to."

They wandered over to the railing of the pier and stared into the dark ocean. A seagull flapped down next to them and started squawking for crusts, even though they'd barely had a bite each. Flash tore off a little piece of his pizza and tossed it to the bird. "His parents probably told him to eat at the fancy restaurant, too."

"Do people ever get on you for, you know, your parents having money? And liking restaurants like that and everything?" Emerson asked. She was thinking about Devane and how the girl always seemed to come up with something to say about Emerson's family being rich.

"At school, no. Pretty much everybody's parents have a ton of cash, or they wouldn't be at my school." He shrugged. "Other places, like . . . other places . . . I get some attitude. Like I'm weak 'cause everything's been handed to me."

Like his hip-hop class, clearly, Emerson thought.

"Why? Do people treat you differently?" Flash asked.

"Sometimes it seems like they trust me less. Like I'm so much different on the inside, just because my clothes cost more, or because I live in a different neighborhood," Emerson admitted.

"Trust you less . . . are we talking about what we're not supposed to be talking about?" Flash asked.

"Sorry," Emerson said. "I was trying to talk about it without talking about it. But only because I can't stop thinking about it."

"Okay, we need the Ferris wheel sooner than I thought. Come on. We can walk and eat. We're very coordinated."

Emerson took a bite of her pizza as they walked toward the bright lights of the big wheel. It was the centerpiece of the pier. She couldn't wait to get on it and start soaring and looping through the night. Maybe Flash was right. Maybe at least while she was on the wheel she wouldn't be able to think of *anything.* That would be so cool. Her brain felt like it was about to overheat.

"You get in line. I'll grab the tix." Flash flashed her a smile as he veered off toward one of the little ticket booths. Emerson joined the group waiting for a turn on the Ferris wheel. It was popular—it seemed like half the people on the pier wanted a ride.

Flash jogged up to her a minute later. "I got a lot. Because I had that dinner money. But mostly because we might want to ride a bunch of times. I like to try and stay on the wheel until I get stuck at the top once. Sometimes the guy running it will let me keep going without getting off. Otherwise, I just tear around to the back of the line as soon as I get off. You up for it?"

"Definitely." Emerson hoped it took a million rides to get one where their basket—the Ferris wheel at the pier had big baskets, not the usual two-person seats—got stuck at the top. It would take that long for her brain to cool down. Plus, it would be fun having all that time to spend up in the air with Flash. If they were heading toward a boyfriend-girlfriend kind of thing, what was more boyfriend-girlfriendish than riding a Ferris wheel together?

An electronic version of some Mozart piece, Emerson wasn't sure which, began to play and Flash pulled out his cell phone. "One sec," he told Emerson. He answered the phone. "Yo, Flash here!"

The smile fell off his face. "This isn't the best time to talk. I thought we all agreed that—" His eyebrows came together in a frown as he listened. "One sec."

Flash lowered the phone and turned to Emerson. "I need to take this. I'll be back before you get to the front of the line."

"Is everything okay?" Emerson asked.

He didn't answer. He was moving away from her too fast. Emerson watched as he stopped near one of those gypsy fortune-teller games that spat out a card with a fortune on it after you fed the machine fifty cents. Flash was facing mostly away from her, but a little of the machine's yellow glow caught the side of his face, and he looked upset. He started to pace back and forth, just a few steps in each direction.

What's going on? she wondered. *Why did he take the call over there? Did something bad happen? Or just something he really doesn't want me to hear?*

Flash whipped around and headed toward her, closing his phone as he walked. Emerson looked up at the Ferris wheel, trying to give the impression that she hadn't been watching him.

"That was a guy from my biology class. We're doing this project together," Flash said when he reached Emerson. "He's mad because he thinks I haven't been doing my share, because of getting ready for the competition and everything. So he says I have to go over to his house and help him tonight."

He's so lying, Emerson thought. *He can't even look at me, he's lying so hard.* But what was she supposed to say? *Good Manners 101: When someone says they want to leave a place, you say of course.* Whether that someone was a big fat liar or not.

"Of course," Emerson said.

"Thanks. I hope you're not too disappointed," Flash

answered.

Great. Now he's using the Good Manners rulebook, too. I thought we were past that, Emerson thought.

"You know what?" Flash said.

Emerson was already starting to hate those words. "What?" she asked.

"Maybe it would be better if we took separate taxis, instead of me dropping you off. It would be faster for me, since the motel and my friend's house are in different directions. He lives by me, in Long Beach."

"No problem," Emerson told him. She wasn't going to beg him to spend more time with her.

"Cool," Flash answered. He rushed her out to a taxi stand about a block away from the pier. He opened the door for her and made sure the driver knew exactly where he needed to go. "See you tomorrow," Flash said as he slammed the door.

Emerson turned around to wave—he hadn't actually given her time to say the words "good-bye." But Flash was already climbing into the cab behind hers. As Emerson's taxi pulled out into the street, Flash's taxi pulled out behind it.

"Um, I don't live here, so I don't know my way around that well, but if we were going to Long Beach, would we be getting on this freeway?" Emerson asked a few blocks later, when the driver approached a freeway entrance.

"Nope. Other direction. I know all the freeways around

here can get confusing," the driver answered.

Huh. Either Flash's taxi driver was confused—and taxi drivers didn't usually get confused about directions—or Flash wasn't going to his friend's house.

Emerson's stomach tightened into a pretzel. Her motel was near the auditorium where the nationals were being held. Could Flash be going there? Had he been talking to someone from the Shoowops on his cell before? Were they planning something?

She didn't want to be so suspicious. But Flash had started acting like a freak. All of a sudden saying he had to help on a biology project—on the night before their big competition. Who did any kind of homework then? And now he wasn't going anywhere near where he said he was going. Emerson pulled out her own cell and dialed her motel room.

Sophie answered, so Emerson felt like she was getting a little lucky. It could have been Devane. "Hey, it's Em," she said. "I don't know if I'm right, but I think the Shoowops might be up to something at the auditorium. I could be being completely crazy, so I don't want to tell everybody. But do you think you could maybe sneak out and meet me over there?"

Sophie said yes. Emerson knew she would. She could count on Sophie no matter what. Sophie was a true friend. And she was willing to do just about anything.

"Change of plans," Emerson told the driver. "I need to

go to the Redondo Beach Performing Arts Center instead."

"You're the boss," the driver told her.

When they were across the street from the center, Emerson said, "Actually, here is good. You don't need to get me right in front." In fact, that would be bad. She didn't want to run into Flash—if this was even where he was headed. She'd lost sight of his cab some time ago.

"You're the boss," the driver repeated. Emerson handed him the fare, plus a big tip. She felt like he was on her side, even though all he'd done was drive her where she'd asked him to, which was his job.

"Thanks," she said. Then she climbed out of the car and shut the door quietly behind her.

Emerson didn't see anyone in front of the center—at least, not until she crossed the street. Then Sophie appeared out of the shadows along the side of the building. Followed by everyone else in Hip Hop Kidz.

"Sorry," Sophie said. "I'm not that good at the sneaking. I got caught, and . . ." She shrugged.

"Okay, this is what we're going to do," Devane said as soon as Emerson showed up. She hadn't even wanted to wait for the girl—there was no time to spare—but Sophie and a bunch of the others had insisted. "We go check everything the Shoowops could have sabotaged and fix it.

Then whatever they did to us, we do something twice as bad to them."

"We don't even know if they did anything," Emerson protested.

"I thought you were on our side. I thought that's why you called," Max said.

"I am. And it is. But I didn't call because I was positive the Shoowops were planning something against us—just that I thought they might be," Emerson answered.

"Fine. If we don't find anything, we don't do anything. But if they decided to throw down with us, we fight back. Agreed?" Devane asked.

"You don't even have to ask," M.J. answered.

"I'm there. I'm ready to kick booty!" Max exclaimed.

Devane looked at Emerson and raised one eyebrow. Emerson reluctantly nodded.

"Okay, then. No one backs out now." Devane led the way into the auditorium lobby. It was quiet. So quiet that the stillness felt like it had weight that was pressing down on her.

"They must be getting ready to close up," ill papi whispered.

"Yeah. Let's get backstage before we're spotted." Devane entered the theater, then walked all the way down the aisle and straight up the short flight of stairs that led to the stage. She could hear the soft footsteps of the group behind her.

Lots of soft footsteps. All she could hope was that whoever was left inside was busy doing . . . something.

Ka-thunk. The lights in the theater behind her went out.

Ka-thunk. The stage lights overhead went out.

Ka-thunk. The backstage lights went out.

Devane was surrounded by darkness.

CHaPtER 13

"Uh-oh," someone said softly. Emerson wasn't even sure who. It was definitely too dark to tell.

"We better get out of here," somebody else whispered. Chloe, Emerson was pretty sure. "Or we might end up staying the night. I think the place is about to get locked up."

"Did anyone—"

"—bring a flashlight?"

The twins. Definitely, Emerson decided.

"I have one on my key chain." Emerson pulled her keys out of her purse and clicked on the tiny but high-powered little light.

"Nice," M.J. said.

"Fridge want," Fridge added.

"Let's get out of here," Rachel begged.

"I want to look around for a minute," Devane answered as she walked backstage.

Emerson followed. The beam from her tiny flashlight jumped around because she couldn't stop her hand from shaking. It flickered from the wall, to a mirror, to a face, to the floor. She had to bite down on the inside of her cheek to keep from screaming. A face. She'd seen a face. And it wasn't anyone from her crew.

She jerked the flashlight back up and sliced it across a row of faces. Shoowop faces. Including Flash.

"Start talking, Gloria. We want to know everything you did to mess with us. Because we're going to find out, anyway," Devane said to her friend.

"I can't believe you're here," Flash said to Emerson. "I've been telling everyone that there was no way you would sabotage us. That you were different from the rest of your group."

"Me?" Emerson gasped. "I'm only here because you're here, Flash. You lied to me. I figured out you were coming here instead of going to your friend's house, and I had to find out why. So tell me why. Come up with one good reason, a reason that makes sense, and I'll believe you. But I know you can't."

"You don't trust me at all, do you?" Flash demanded. "I thought we . . . I don't know what I thought."

"You expect me to just trust you after you lie right to my face?" Emerson shot back.

"Yes!" Flash told her. "That call I got at the pier—it was from Vince," Flash said. "He told me that he found out that someone from our crew had taken those insane socks.

I guess someone had overheard M.J. talking about them at the party."

Emerson shot a look at Devane. Who was not looking at her.

"Anyway, I realized that even though the Shoowops actually started the whole thing between our groups, a lot of people on my crew were wanting revenge for the mirror thing—"

"The mirror thing was fair. You shoved. We shoved back," M.J. cut in.

"Whatever." Flash kept talking to Emerson, and Emerson only. "I came down here to stop any more stupidity. I got here before anyone did any damage. I would have handled the whole thing, if you'd just trusted me."

"I would have trusted you to handle it if you'd told me the truth," Emerson insisted.

"I want to check things out for myself. I want to—" Fridge was interrupted by a *thud.*

"I think someone might be coming up the stage stairs," Rachel whispered.

Flash picked up a baseball bat that The Team had used in its routine and rolled it across the stage. Emerson heard footsteps start in the direction the bat rolled.

"Come on." Flash hurried over to the back exit.

The door was locked.

"We're trapped," Slider hissed.

Zach stepped up to the door, pulled out a small pocket knife, and stuck the blade into the lock. He twisted the knife. Jiggled it. Twisted again. And the door opened with a squeak.

Emerson and the others ran. They didn't stop until they were a block away from the auditorium. "If we'd been caught in there, we would have been booted from the nationals," Flash announced. "To risk getting booted to get a better chance at winning—that's seriously stupid, I think."

"Me too," Emerson agreed. She wasn't happy with Flash. At all. But she thought he was right.

"You're on his side?" Devane asked.

"I'm on the side of us staying in the competition," Emerson told her. "And when did Hip Hop Kidz decide to become cheaters?" she continued. "If that's the only way we can win, I want to quit right now. I don't even want to wait until I get back to Florida and my parents make me."

"Yeah," Sophie said. "If we're going to get scuzzy, I don't want to be in the group either." Emerson smiled at her. She could always count on Sophie to have her back.

"I don't think we need any extra help to win," ill papi said.

M.J. didn't say anything. Neither did Gloria. Emerson suspected they both really thought they *did* need their good luck to win.

"Neither do we," Princess said.

Devane snorted. "Have you watched your own tape?"

Max laughed.

Emerson winced. There was going to be another huge blowup right here.

"So it's agreed then?" Flash asked, before everyone could start getting into it again. "A straight-up clean competition?"

"If you give me back the socks," M.J. told him.

"No way," Zach said. "You guys broke Gloria's mirror. We know you did."

"And you can't unbreak it," Slider jumped in. "If we have to go into the competition with the bad luck from the mirror, you guys don't get the lucky socks."

Sophie was glad they'd declared a truce with the Shoowops. It was true what she'd said—she really wouldn't want to stay in the group if they decided to go in for some major trashing of the other crew. The mirror thing was no biggie. It was at about the same level as the socks. A superstition for a superstition.

"Hey, thanks for backing me up tonight," Emerson said, falling into step with Sophie as they walked to the motel.

"You were saying all the things I was thinking. Flash, too," Sophie told her. "Are you guys . . . What do you think is going to happen with you guys?"

"He lied right to my face. That's big," Emerson said. "How do you keep being friends with someone after that?"

"Yeah."

"Crazy night, huh?" Emerson asked. "Sammi seems especially upset. Do you think she's okay?"

Sophie glanced around until she spotted her sister in the group. She was holding hands with Ky, but Sophie caught her looking over her shoulder in ill papi's direction. Em was right. Sammi did not look like a happy girl.

I practically lied to her face that night she tried to talk to me about Ky and ill papi, Sophie thought, spirals of guilt twisting through her. *Not telling her what I knew about ill papi was pretty much as bad as lying.*

"I'm going to go talk to her for a minute," Sophie said. "I'll be back." She trotted past a few people until she reached Sammi. "Hey, Ky. I need to borrow my sis."

"As long as you give her back," Ky answered.

Sophie wasn't actually sure she'd be able to. So she just smiled at him.

"What's up?" Sammi asked, when she and Sophie had fallen a little behind the crowd.

"You're my sister," Sophie began.

"Yeeesss," Sammi agreed, in a kind of no-duh way.

"So I want things to be good between us. More than good. I guess I started thinking about it with all the madness between the Kidz and the Shoowops. I don't know." Sophie rushed on. "Anyway. There's something I should have told you before. But I'm going to tell you now, so I hope it's okay. It's not like I was keeping a secret exactly. Except you might think so, but—"

"Soph, it's okay. Whatever it is, just tell me," Sammi said.

"The other night, at the party at Flash's, ill papi told me he likes you. Really *likes* you," Sophie confessed. "He didn't ask me to tell you that or anything. He just told me because he saw you and Ky kissing and I guess it just hit him hard. Basically, he's always liked you."

"But you said he decided not to like anyone. And he turned me down when I asked him to go to the movies with me," Sammi said. She sounded confused—but also excited.

"He's scared," Sophie explained. "I don't think he wants to like anyone. I think he really believes all it does is mess people up. But he likes you. The boy can't help himself." She felt her throat tighten, but she forced herself to go on. "You know you rock, Sammi. I'm surprised, like, trees aren't falling in love with you."

"You like him, too, don't you?" Sammi asked. "And not just as a friend, right?"

Sophie thought about lying. But there'd been too much of that lately. "Yeah," she admitted. "That's probably why I took so long to tell you. I was sort of jealous. Forgive me?"

Sammi knocked shoulders with her. "Of course. And it's not like I'm never jealous of you, you know."

"I'm sure," Sophie muttered.

"It's true. Because you can talk to anyone—old ladies you meet on the bus, little kids, and cute guys. And you can make almost anyone laugh," Sammi explained. "Everyone likes you, Soph. Plus, you're really brave. You'll do anything if you think someone needs you to—even if it makes you look silly, or if you know it's going to hurt. Or course I'm jealous sometimes."

Sophie couldn't say anything. She just . . . couldn't say anything. Sammi was jealous of her sometimes? The top of her head was about to fly off.

"Hey, you're *my* sister, too," Sammi added. "I want things to be great between us. If my getting, you know, closer to ill papi is going to make you feel bad—"

"No. Well, maybe a little. I'm not going to be happy with ill papi liking any girl but me. Except he doesn't feel that way about me, and he's not going to. But he does feel that way about you. So, you should go for it," Sophie said.

Sammi smiled. "Okay, well, maybe I will." She gave Sophie a big hug. "You're the best sister ever."

"You too," Sophie answered.

Sammi felt a huge grin stretch across her face. She couldn't stop it. Ill papi *liked* her!

"Uh, Sammi," Sophie said. "Ky's looking back at us. And

I'm pretty sure he thinks you're smiling at him."

Sammi forced herself to wave at Ky and tried not to let her smile fade. Ky. She'd forgotten all about Ky the whole time she and Soph were talking about ill papi.

That was so not right. Ky was awesome. He really was. And he really liked her. And he wasn't afraid to say it.

Who knew if ill papi would ever be able to actually tell Sammi how he felt? He wasn't even ready to go see a movie with her!

You need to step back and do some hard thinking, Sammi told herself. *Because no matter what you decide, somebody's going to get hurt.*

Maybe you.

CHAPTER 14

This is it, Emerson thought as she watched the group ahead of the Kidz wrap up their routine. *We have two minutes to show the judges and everybody in the audience everything we've got.*

"I just wanted to say good luck."

Emerson jerked her head toward the voice and saw Flash standing next to her. He was getting some non-happy looks from some of her crew, but he ignored them. Emerson ignored them, too. "Thanks. You too." It was the polite response.

He kept standing there, like he wanted to say something else. "I'm really mad at you for lying to me last night!" Emerson blurted out. Not the polite thing to do.

"Yeah. I know. I'm still kind of mad at you for not trusting me. I can't believe you thought I was going to sabotage your crew," Flash answered.

Emerson sighed. "I can see why you'd be mad. But you were in the auditorium in the middle of the night. It looked . . . not so good."

"I get that. That's why I'm only kind of mad," Flash told her. "I think I'll get over it. Do you think you can get over the other thing?"

Out of the corner of her eye, Emerson saw J-Bang take the stage. He began his introduction of the Hip Hop Kidz.

"The lying?" Emerson asked. She felt bad when Flash winced. "Yeah. If you can stop being mad at me, I can stop being mad at you. I do understand why you wanted to keep what the Shoowops were doing to yourself. You were protecting your friends."

"Cool." Flash gave her a lightning fast kiss on the cheek. "I don't know if I should tell you this, because today we're big enemies and everything, but when I was watching you rehearse, I noticed that you take your line just a little bit too far to the left in that section where you, the girl with the red hair, and Sophie move away from the main group. Just a little."

"Oh, yikes. That's not good. I'll try to watch that," Emerson said.

"Straight from my home state, Florida, give it up for the Hip Hop Kidz!" J-Bang shouted out.

"This is it, you guys," Gina told them. "Just do it the way you always do and you'll be fantastic."

The familiar Kanye West beats started up. Emerson had to remind herself to breathe as she watched the Hip Hop Kidz take the stage in pairs. Then she was out there. Under the lights. Half-blinded. But totally alive.

Top rock, drop to flare, bronco it up. Now it was time to take her group left. Emerson cat-walked over, arching her back, releasing, arching. Far enough? A little farther?

Oh, no! She'd messed up. She'd been so busy thinking about exactly how far left to go that she'd kept moving a beat longer than she should. She'd never done that before. And she had to do it today—the day of the nationals. Now her line was definitely too far over.

How much did it show? Could the judges tell her line was in the wrong place? Did the composition look really weird and bad? Had she just blown the nationals?

Don't panic. You'll just mess up more, Emerson told herself as she moved on with the routine. It was time for her solo. The strobing pirouette was almost as familiar as walking to her by now. When she finished, she got a surge of applause. Was her perfection move good enough to compensate for her screwup?

Too late now. Nothing she could do. The most important two minutes of her life were over. She hit the final freeze. *This could be the very last time I'm onstage with the Hip Hop Kidz*. The thought was like being shoved into an icy shower.

You're here now, she told herself, trying to soak in every detail. The way the lights heated her skin. The way adrenaline pumped through her, making her body tingle. The way she could see Soph grinning off to her left. *Yeah, you're here now*, she thought again.

But as she headed offstage, the words "last time" kept thudding through her head. *Had* that been her last time onstage with her crew? And had her mistake cost her friends the chance to move on to the World Hip-Hop Championship?

Devane stood in the wings, watching the Shoowops out on the stage. Gloria and her partner were front and center. Gloria had her knees locked around his neck, and her body stretched out as he spun.

She really is close to Devane-worthy. And the Shoowops, they were very close to Hip Hop Kidz–worthy.

Who was she fooling? The Shoowops were fierce. Devane had no idea who the judges would like more—the Shoowops or the Kidz. Maybe they'd go for the swing stuff the Shoowops brought to hip-hop. Although Emerson did sort of the same thing with ballet.

Devane thought maybe the Kidz were a little more athletic. Moves like M.J.'s jackhammer took major power, and the Shoowops didn't go there in their routine. But the way their guys swung the girls over their heads—it wasn't like you didn't have to be an athlete for that.

Suddenly the crowd was giving it up for the group. More than for the Kidz? A little less? Devane really couldn't tell.

How could the judges make a call after watching a routine that lasted two minutes? The Kidz couldn't show everything they had in two minutes. Two minutes wasn't—

Devane realized that Gloria had stopped near her on her way offstage. Not so near that either of them absolutely had to say something. But close. Devane ignored her and watched J-Bang as he introduced the next group, the Momma's Boys.

Now they *definitely* weren't Shoowop- or Kidz-worthy, Devane quickly decided. How had these people even gotten into the nationals? She heard Gloria give a quiet "hmmm" that made her think Gloria was feeling the same way.

A short boy with curly light brown hair moved center for a solo. Devane didn't care about his moves—he didn't have any. But the guy looked so familiar. Especially the way he was jerking his head back and forth. She gave a bark of laughter when she realized why. "Bobby Martin," she said to Gloria.

"What?" Gloria asked.

"That guy doing the solo looks exactly like Bobby Martin from third grade," Devane explained.

"I don't remember him," Gloria said.

"How can you not remember him? Of course you remember him," Devane told her. "He used to tell dumb jokes every day at lunch. Nobody would laugh but him, 'cause they were that dumb. But Bobby would laugh so hard—"

"That milk would spray out of his nose! I remember,"

Gloria exclaimed.

"What made me think of it was the neck moves that guy's got going on, plus the hair and the shortness," Devane said. "Remember how Bobby's neck would always twitch before the milk spewage?"

"It was so gross!" Gloria agreed. "But at least we knew when to take cover." She looked over at Devane. "We didn't have anybody like Bobby at my other school." She hesitated, then added, "And there was definitely no one like you."

"Well, there is only one Devane," Devane answered. But she knocked shoulders with Gloria. She wanted her friend to know she was only teasing.

"Yeah. I missed you tons," Gloria said. "You were always so much fun."

"I missed you, too," Devane admitted. "So I guess that means we're still friends, huh?" Now that both crews had finished their performances, it was hard to feel angry at Gloria or any of the Shoowops anymore. The Kidz and the Shoowops had both gotten a little out of hand.

Gloria smiled. "Still friends," she answered. "But I still want to win this thing," she warned.

Devane grinned. "You must not remember me that well if you don't know that I never stopped wanting to win for a second."

"I'll talk to my team," Gloria said. "We should celebrate together tonight—no matter what. Do you think your crew

146

will be down with that?"

"They do what I tell them," Devane joked. "I'll ask Gina if we can have you guys over at the motel. The pool isn't as big as the one at Flash's, but there's enough room for all of us."

Please let us be in the top three, Emerson silently begged as she waited backstage for the judges to make their decision. *Let us at least go on to world, even though I messed up. I'm not ready to stop being a Hip Hop Kid yet.*

"You're thinking about the forbidden topic, aren't you?" a voice asked from behind her. A voice that sounded suspiciously like it belonged to a certain boy she still wasn't sure if she should speak to. A certain boy she was dying to speak to, but nevertheless hesitated in front of.

Emerson turned around to see if her suspicions were correct. There, facing her, was the sweet face of the handsomest boy she knew.

"It's not forbidden anymore," she answered.

"Yeah, well . . ." Flash hesitated, then continued in a rush. "I just wanted to say that whatever happens, whoever wins, I don't want it to change anything with us. Whoever gets it, you're still my girlfriend, okay?"

A burst of happiness surged through Emerson. And for a moment, she forgot about the mess-up and the fact that the consequences to the mess-up were about to be determined.

"I didn't know I was."

"Oh. Well. Is it okay? I mean, do you want to be?" Flash asked, staring down at her with his forehead all wrinkly.

"Yes. Whoever wins. Or loses," Emerson told him. "That shouldn't affect what happens between us. But even though I'm totally your girlfriend, I think I need to be with my crew right now. I want to be with them when J-Bang announces the winners."

"I get that. I should be over with the Shoowops," Flash said. "But Gloria and Devane are working up some kind of party. So I'll see you there?"

"Absolutely," Emerson told him, beaming. She just hoped her team would want to party after the winners were announced.

She hurried into the wings and found a spot next to Sophie. Devane glanced over, and for a second Emerson was sure Devane was going to ask her why she wasn't over with the Shoowops.

But Devane gave a little smile and said, "Yeah, this is where you belong."

It was what Devane had said to her after they'd both gotten into the Performance Group. Well, not right after, but after Devane had accepted that Emerson could really dance. And that she really cared about the group.

"I think so, too," Emerson replied.

"Sorry I forgot that for a while," Devane said.

"J-Bang's getting onstage. He's going to announce the winners!" Chloe exclaimed.

"It's okay," Emerson told Devane.

Devane reached out her hand and Emerson grabbed it. Sophie grabbed Emerson's other hand.

"All right. I know you aren't all out there just to look at my pretty face," J-Bang called out. "You want to know who took the nationals, don't you?"

"Uh, yeah," Sophie said as the crowd burst into applause.

"All right, all right, coming in at third place, we've got the crew that mixed up martial arts and hip-hop and knocked us all onto the floor—"

"That's definitely not us," Emerson said. Sophie and Devane both gave her hand a squeeze.

"The Shadow Boxers!" J-Bang called out.

"Did you guys see how I messed up in that one part where I take my group over to the left? I kept going a little too long," Emerson confessed as the Shadow Boxers went out to get their trophy.

"I didn't notice," Sophie said.

But Sophie was in her group, so Emerson figured she probably did. She was just being nice—so Em wouldn't feel bad. But if the Hip Hop Kidz didn't make it to world because of her, Emerson was going to feel more than bad. She was going to feel like the worst human being in the world.

"Coming in at number two," J-Bang cried. "A group whose athletic ability and outstanding choreography impressed us all."

"He could be talking about almost any crew," Sophie said.

Including us, Emerson thought. Her toes started to cramp and she realized that she'd been curling them inside her shoes.

"This crew is always fun to watch," J-Bang continued.

"Fun. That's what he said about us at the regionals," Devane burst out. "Is he talking about us? No way, we don't deserve second."

But do the Shoowops? Emerson wondered. There was no way they wouldn't get one of the top two spots. They'd been amazing today. None of them had made one wrong step—as far as she'd been able to tell.

"A crew with enough power and energy to light up the whole state of California," J-Bang continued.

"That could also be any group. This is driving me crazy," Sammi said.

"Let's give it up for these folks coming straight from my old stomping ground—the Hip Hop Kidz!" J-Bang hollered.

We would have gotten first if it hadn't been for me, Emerson thought.

Then Sophie was hugging her. And so was Devane. And the whole group was rushing the stage. Maddy and Gina, too. Maddy took the trophy from J-Bang and held it over her head, then passed it to Gina. Gina handed it to Fridge, who passed it to Max, who handed it to Allan, who gave it to his twin, who turned it over to Rachel, who passed it to Becca, who passed it to Sammi, who gave it to Sophie, who presented it to Devane with a flourish, who gave it to Emerson with a grin.

"We're going on to world!" Devane cried.

True, Emerson thought as she followed the group offstage—where she handed the trophy to ill papi so he had a chance to touch it. *Making it to world is the most important thing. And now I get to be a Hip Hop Kid a little longer. I get to be part of this crew for a few more days.* She started to feel a little better.

"Did you even hear that?" Sophie demanded. "J-Bang just announced that your boyfriend's crew won first place!"

"I guess Gloria's broken mirror wasn't that unlucky after all," Becca said.

"And we did pretty well without M.J.'s socks," Chloe added.

"We definitely smell better," Fridge agreed.

"My jackhammer didn't need any help," M.J. told them all. "Did you see it? It was smokin'. I might start performing barefoot. Forget socks altogether."

That got him a bunch of groans. He grinned.

"I think we should make the party tonight a Shoowops

victory bash!" Devane cried.

"What?" Fridge demanded. "Have you gone freaky?"

"No, I think they deserve a party now," Devane answered. "Because we are going to triumph over them at world!"

"Yeah!" Emerson yelled, as loud and not-politely as she could. She was going to have another chance to give her all for her team. And she promised herself she wouldn't let them down at world.

The Hip Hop Kidz would become the World Hip-Hop Champions—no matter what it took!

DEF-iniTions

Boxing: A move where the dancer creates box shapes, usually with his/her arms.

Clowning: A mix of popping, locking, break dancing, and African tribal dance.

Eggbeater: A sustained backspin with legs in the air and hands high on the hips.

Freeze: The dancer stops in the middle of a move and holds the position.

Hinging: A style where the dancer makes his/her joints look like hinges that can be controlled by other body parts.

Jackhammer: The dancer is down on the ground with the body stretched out, using one hand to hop in a circle.

Krumping: Fusion of clowning and hip-hop.

Locking: A jerky style where the dancer moves through a series of ultra-quick poses.

Popping: A style where the dancer moves through poses in a more fluid way than in locking.

Slide: Sliding across the floor on some part of the body.

Strobing: The dancer takes an everyday motion and makes it look as though it's being done under a strobe light.

Top rock: Four-step, four-beat basic dance that many hip-hoppers use to launch into more complicated moves.

Tutting: The dancer hits a pose that uses the wrists, arms, and shoulders to create right angles (King Tut–style), then moves almost immediately into another pose.

Waves: A move that uses muscle flexes and releases to make it look like a wave is traveling through the dancer's body.

Hey, y'all,

Hip Hop Kidz plays a major role in my life. The program has
taught me so much—not just about dancing and performing, but
also about being a better person. For instance, I've learned that if
I keep a good attitude during the good, the bad, and the ugly, then
I will have a better chance at making it in the industry. The Kidz
in this book found out that keeping their cool and not giving in to
cheating at the regionals was better than risking getting caught,
even if it meant competing against a group with mad skills like the
Shoowops. Like ill papi said, the Kidz didn't need any extra help to
win—because if the dancing is fly enough, it will speak for itself.
Sometimes doing the right thing seems harder than doing the
thing that will get you where you want to go, but in the end, you
feel better if you can respect yourself.

Richard, age 14